Between the Sheets

LIV RANCOURT
author of *Forever and Ever, Amen*

CRIMSON
ROMANCE

F+W Media, Inc.

Published by
Crimson Romance
an imprint of F+W Media, Inc.
10151 Carver Road, Suite 200
Blue Ash, OH 45242. U.S.A.
www.crimsonromance.com

ISBN 10: 1-4405-8484-2
ISBN 13: 978-1-4405-8484-8
eISBN 10: 1-4405-8485-0
eISBN 13: 978-1-4405-8485-5

Cover art © 123RF/Raya Hristova

This story is dedicated to my three favorite music teachers, Mrs. Arizzi, Miss Sunde, and Mrs. Berry. I'll forever be grateful for the ways you've influenced my life.

I'd like to thank my fabulous beta readers Amanda, Ruth, Rhay, and Debbie. You guys keep all my ducks in a row, for sure. I'd also like to thank Tara, Jess, and Julie at Crimson. As always, you guys are fantastic to work with! And finally, I'd like to thank my oh-so-patient husband and kids, who put up with my absentee status while I got this baby finished.

Chapter 1

The guys on my softball team liked to talk a big story, but Krista and I were the ones who hung out the longest after our games. Thursday night at O'Brien's meant happy hour until nine and Irish music until closing. Well before eight o'clock, the last of the ballplayers left us alone at a debris-covered table, with the band in the corner playing a reel.

"They bailed on us again," Krista said, raising her voice to be heard over the pipes and fiddle. Friends since college, we'd gone through the same music ed program. Now I taught grade school kids while she had a job in a middle school. It gave her a hipper aura, which I often envied. Like right now, for instance.

I stacked empty pint glasses, and the hurricane candle on our rickety table flickered. "We're the only ones who don't have to go to work in the morning."

"We do too, Maggie Jeanne." She snorted like I'd insulted her dignity and raised her glass in toast. "To choir camp."

"Geez, don't call it choir camp." I clinked my pint glass against hers with a laugh threaded with sarcasm. "And don't call me Maggie Jeanne."

"Oh, pardon me. To a successful, um, Western Washington Choral Directors Annual Retreat."

I let my glass tip forward, coming close to pouring beer in her lap. "Whatever."

"I could have said…what would it be? W-W-C-D-A-R? DubDub-Cee-Dar?"

"Give it up." I shrugged, rocking my head in time with the drum's bass beat. I knew the musicians in this band and planned to join in if anyone started step-dancing. Or elbow my way on stage and grab the harp. Or take a turn on the bodhrán. "I can't imagine anything happening this time that hasn't happened the last two or three years."

"What are you talking about?" Krista whipped out her phone, which may or may not have buzzed with a text message. She maintained a man-harem big enough to make my eyes cross.

"The weather is gorgeous and we're going to be out of town for three nights." She waved her empty glass at the crowd. "There is *no end* to the adventure we could have."

"Adventure? With a bunch of music teachers?" I topped the empty nacho tray with used snack plates.

She half stood and leaned over the table to point in the direction of my belly. "Sit up straight and lift your shirt."

"No way." I clutched at my grubby softball jersey, the soft yellow hem smudged with red clay from a head-first dive into second base.

"You've got bricks under there, girlfriend. I've seen them."

"So?"

"You're too cute to be single. Half the men in this bar would do you right now." She sat down with a smug grin, like she'd just nailed me with a killer argument.

"Yeah, the drunk ones," I muttered into my beer. Whenever Krista played her "Maggie needs a man" rap, it blasted my ego—and my heart—like a storm of irritated bees.

She brushed off my rebuttal with a *whatever* eye roll.

"Anyway," I said, hoping to put this conversation to bed, "all the guys at the retreat will all be married or gay or both."

Those conversations didn't usually end well.

The waitress slipped through the clot of grown up frat boys surrounding our table to see if we wanted another pitcher of beer. I said no. Krista said yes. I glared. She caved.

At least the debate saved me from Krista's enthusiasm for a couple of minutes.

"You know what I love?" Krista started yapping as soon as the waitress left. "The feeling when a guy first slides himself in, you know?" She faked a shiver. "You might not remember this, but the first long thrust, when everything is tight and you have to work it in. It's so…yum."

Aw, now she's playing the sexy card. I blinked once. Twice. I fought to keep my eyes from widening and bit down on the tip of my tongue. Hard. She did the fake shiver thing again, her chin jittering on the inhale. I couldn't help myself. I laughed, coming very close to snorting beer out my nose.

"You are so full of shit."

"And you *so* need to get laid." Satisfied with making her point, Krista adjusted her purple-framed glasses and took a hit from her beer. Between the blocky frames and the hard edge of her bangs, she should have a pocket protector and a compass in her pocket instead of lipstick and an iPhone. Next to her edgy style, my wispy blond hair and twice-broken nose said sidekick. Jock. Tomboy.

"You're not denying it," she said, tapping the table with a blunt fingernail.

If we dug into all the reasons I preferred to limit guys to friendship, we'd have to take this little discussion to a therapist's couch.

"Maggie …" She dragged out the word.

"What? You're right. I need to get laid." I raised my glass to nearly eye level as if inspecting the amber color for flaws. "Is that what you want to hear?"

"Only if you mean it."

I sipped some beer. Did I mean it this time? It had been a while. Five years, three months, and four days, actually.

Not that I'd been keeping track.

The band swung into a hornpipe, the bodhrán laying down an easy rhythm. A girl started step-dancing near the stage, and then another joined in. If I got up and danced, I could avoid the conversation entirely.

On the other hand, she was right. I needed to get laid.

Because five years, three months, and four days ago, I'd been wearing a white lace dress when my groom called to say he was on his way to Los Angeles.

Alone.

Krista made kissy-lips, which meant she had an idea. "The Blues Revivalists are playing in Langley on Sunday night. If the music teachers strike out, we could head over so you can try with the rock 'n' rollers."

I chewed a pinky nail, delaying my answer. Maybe I finally felt strong enough.

A tall man with shaggy brown hair sat down at the table next to ours. Krista tipped her nose in his direction and let her gaze drift significantly. I ignored her, studying the *Lord of the Rings* posters on the wall.

"Sometimes you gotta open yourself up a little, you know. Try something new to get what you want," she said.

"Okay. Fine. I have a goal for the weekend."

Krista clapped her hands like a little girl. "Goodie!"

A burble of giddiness broke free from somewhere deep. I was going to get laid. Didn't know with whom, and didn't know when, but I was going to do it.

Chapter 2

The next morning, it took a little while to shake off the crusty edges from a night of beer and music. My first waking thought was, *Krista dared me to get laid and I said I'd do it. Alrighty, then.* I'd also volunteered to drive, because between the two of us, I was the one most likely to be starting from her own bed.

After a quick exchange of texts to confirm her location, Krista climbed into my CRV clutching a travel mug, her face wrapped in a pair of black Ray-Bans. She smelled like apples and sex, and though I couldn't see her eyes, she could see me and had no qualms about sharing her opinion.

"Your shirt," she said, flicking a finger in my direction. "It's baggy."

Something about her tone made me nervous. "It's clean."

"It's boring. How are you going to get laid if you hide the goodies under a sack?"

Apparently she hadn't forgotten my goal either. I pulled out onto Lake City Way, certain Krista's present mood wasn't going to help my hangover. At. All.

We drove in silence until Alderwood Mall came into sight. "Don't miss the exit," she said.

"We've got a ways to go to get to Mukilteo."

She glared at me over top of her Ray-Bans. "We're stopping at Target first. If you packed for comfort instead of cute, you'll never get any action." She used her bossy-teacher voice, oblivious to my eye-rolling and halfhearted harrumph.

Okay, quick decision. I could hold tight to my values and keep driving north, or I could concede defeat and let her help me choose an outfit that might get me laid. The throbbing in my head was somehow echoed by something further south, and I could see the big red logo from the freeway. "I do need some moisturizer."

As soon as we hit Target, she dragged me toward the women's clothing.

"The moisturizer's over there," I said, pointing in what I hoped was the right direction.

"We can go get some as soon as you try this on," she shoved a cobalt blue sleeveless dress in my hands—"and this"—a paisley print peasant blouse in greens and lavender—"and this."

The last item was stretchy and black and short enough to be a skirt, because as a dress it would let way too much Maggie hang out the back end. Krista turned to another rack, and just as quickly I hung up the black thing. And then I picked it up again. I was a tomboy, not an idiot. Maybe something short, black, and stretchy would change things for me.

The shopping frenzy didn't take long. Despite the low odds of actually breaking my drought, I had a moment of maturity and wheeled our cart through the contraception aisle on our way to the checkout. After all, low was not the same as zero, and Lord knew any condoms I owned would be well past their shelf life. The *Cosmo* magazine Krista tossed in my basket, however, almost broke my resolve. Grown-ups didn't read *Cosmo*. Right?

Of course, her rah-rah enthusiasm did a better job than coffee to clear my head.

We pulled onto the freeway toward the ferry dock at Mukilteo and she twisted in her seat, giving me a smile that would have flustered the Cheshire Cat.

"You're wearing a dress. You're seriously wearing a dress, and you look hot."

I plucked at my dark green hoodie, a sure sign of embarrassment. It didn't quite match my brand-new topaz flowered sun dress, but the late August morning was too cool for a halter top.

Krista lifted her sunglasses. "Blue is a good color with your eyes." She leaned forward to peer at my feet. "Wish we had time to go for pedicures."

"No way." My feet were so calloused from daily trail runs, I'd never let anyone near them with nail polish.

We cruised north on the freeway and she reclined her seat, the coffee mug near her cheek, all but purring with satisfaction. "Soon as I wake up a bit more," she said, "we're going to have a little strategy session."

Wake up more?

An hour later I parked on the ferry ramp and we climbed the corrugated steel steps to the passenger deck. At just after ten on a Friday morning, the ferry wasn't crowded, even though we were still in vacation season. Rows of orange vinyl booths sat perpendicular to long windows, overlooking sapphire water, the surface sparkling like mica as small waves danced in the breeze.

I picked a spot where the sun turned the seat's vinyl a warm tangerine. Krista plunked down next to me and tossed the *Cosmo* in my lap. "Read," she said.

My morals were being tested, but the splashy pink dress worn by the cover model was kind of cute. Her smile dared me to— do something, and the headline in the upper left corner tweaked my curiosity. *Be a Sex Diva: Naughty Tricks Men Crave.* While the combination of daylight and sobriety assured me the odds of practicing any kind of naughty tricks at the choir director's retreat were low at best, it never hurt to expand the repertoire.

And my repertoire was woefully rusty.

Fifteen minutes later I'd figured out *Cosmo* was *so* not the magazine for me. I didn't want to dress like Angelina Jolie or learn how to apply black Amy Winehouse-style eyeliner copied from a 1950s Barbie Doll. I worked out often enough my stomach was already flat, thanks. If anything, my boyish body needed *more* curves, but none of the articles went there.

I came to the article promising to turn me into a sex diva. *Crazy.* Halfway down the page, one of the bold-type headings demanded I *Flick His Frenulum.* I vowed to flick the next one I saw, once I figured out where it was located. Apparently it would fire up his treasure trail, the line of hair running south from his bellybutton. The article said a real diva should take the initiative and undress her man. And I could imagine doing that exactly *never.* The next page suggested the standing doggie-style position would bring me to the highest heights.

O-kay.

The whole thing had me all twisted up, excitement and fear and desire making like ribbon candy in my belly. I tried to picture the kind of man I'd want behind me for standing doggie style. My ex came to mind, but right about the time the flood of bad memories started, Krista interrupted me with a sharp poke to the ribs.

"Check him out," she said, her voice barely audible.

A man leaned against the railing at the front of the boat. He stared out at the water, taking lazy drags off the butt of a cigarette. Since he mostly had his back to us, I felt free to check him out.

Yum. He wore a pair of faded jeans and a light green T-shirt. He turned to the right, giving us a profile shot and showing off a pair of wire-rimmed glasses. His toned forearm had the freckled, light toast color redheads get in the sun. He wasn't a true carrot-top; more like a sandy red, and his short hair could have used a trim. His beard, too, was a day or so into scruffy.

A black tattoo circled his arm just below the hem of his sleeve, calling attention to the swell of his bicep. I closed the magazine and sat forward, trying to get a better look at the tat, when Krista grabbed my elbow.

"There is no way." I spoke without turning my head or moving my lips, even though my twisted candy core started to melt. "Because even if he turns out, by some miracle, to be a music teacher, I couldn't string sentences together in front of someone so incredibly handsome."

She gave my elbow a shake. "If you get the chance, you are totally going to hit that."

I shoved the magazine at her, hoping the Ginger God didn't turn around and notice my blush.

Krista had always been the optimistic one.

Chapter 3

Between the dull rumble of the ferry's engines and Krista's strategizing, my hangover head was overwhelmed in something less than twelve minutes. To combat them both, I dug out my mp3 player and let my favorite band, Albannach, cut loose with a sound so hot it all but melted my ear buds. If I turned the music loud enough, I couldn't hear Krista's pointed sighs.

Funny how the dull ache in my head could handle Scottish pipes, but not her "how to get a man" pep talk.

Out our window, a gull took a couple of lazy flaps with his wings, then dropped toward the water. He must have missed his intended victim, because his beak was empty when he came up. *Good for you, fishie!*

When the other passengers packed up, Krista and I followed. We were halfway down the stairs to the car deck when the high-pitched grind from the engines told us the ferry captain had thrown on the brakes, and we scurried the rest of the way.

"Are you ready for this?" Krista asked, buckling herself into my CRV.

I pulled the earbuds out and tossed the player in my bag. Just outside our window, another gull made a dive for the waves and came up with breakfast. He flew past, the fish's tail flipping in defeat. I knew how it felt. "What are my options, again?"

"You could have a little fun." She lifted her shades to wink at me. "Or you could punk out."

Her evil smile let me know which one she'd choose.

The rolling two-lane road took us past miniature farms, their space limited by the size of the island, then dumped us into the forest. The retreat was held at Lorreson Lodge, a three-story wood building fronted by a circular driveway and flanked by a half-circle of cabins. The front door faced the forest and behind the lodge was ocean beach.

The main entrance rose two full stories, anchored by a huge stone fireplace with a slate hearth. To the right of the fireplace a door led to the dining hall, and to the left was a stairway to the guest rooms on the second and third floors. Krista and I had reserved one of the cabins, figuring we might need an escape hatch. Bundling my things out of my CRV, I was grateful for her foresight.

A card table had been set to the left of the front door as a check-in point for the conference attendees. We got ourselves signed in, dumped our gear in the cabin, and went to the orientation session. The room was about two-thirds full, and I couldn't help myself; I spent the entire ninety minutes assessing my fellow conference attendees for their romantic possibilities.

Well, the male ones, anyway.

They finally cut us loose, and Krista and I shuffled along the sandy path to our two-room cabin. We had one of the lucky ones facing the beach, which was cool, but still—if we held hands, Krista and I could touch all the walls in the main room at once. It held two bunks, a desk, and a folding chair, and the bathroom was so tiny I wasn't sure I'd be able to turn around in the shower.

"'*Keeping your program afloat*'? What a lame-ass title. Their 'advocacy skills' were rehashed common sense and a lot of wishful thinking." Krista pushed the cabin door open wide, and a blast of late-afternoon sun highlighted the dusty sand our feet kicked up.

I landed hard on my bunk, the coils under the mattress giving a perfunctory whimper of protest. "Because starting off a conference with an hour-and-a-half discussion on how to keep your job is always uplifting."

"Damn."

Not exactly the response I was expecting, and Krista's thumbs began a furious flurry over her phone.

"What?" I asked.

She tossed her phone on the bed. "Effing J-Bone says he can't come Sunday night."

"J-Bone?" I reached behind my neck for the ties holding my halter top up. "You're dating a guy named J-Bone?"

"Well, everybody's gotta have something they're good at." She propped herself up on her elbows and gave me a naughty wink. "And don't even think about taking your dress off."

I was saved from having to respond by her phone's chirp. By the time she refocused on me, I'd untied the dress and was digging through my duffel bag for a pair of shorts.

"Nope. No way." She swung her legs around to sit on the edge of the bed. "Social hour is next, and you're not going dressed as a shortstop."

"First base."

"Whatever."

Irritation drop-kicked my sense of humor out the window and I planted my fists on my hips. The front of my halter dress flopped forward, but I was too pissed to care. "Did you see anyone out there who would possibly care what I am wearing?"

"Yes." Her phone chirped. "Wait a sec." She grabbed it. "And put a shirt on. Your titties are bugging me."

I expelled a bunch of frustration in a sigh for the ages and dropped onto the bed. I didn't exactly tie the halter, but at least I tossed the straps over my shoulders.

Krista finished her text and raised an eyebrow at me. "P. Kirk Ringdahl is here."

The head of our local teacher's consortium, Kirk Ringdahl, starred in his own show. His breezy confidence was born of being one of the only unattached males in any group of music teachers, a status elevating him to the center of attention.

Sure, I'd seen him. And chosen to ignore him. "So?"

"So? He's straight and single and—"

"If you say he's handsome, I'm going to puke." And I meant it. Seriously. My day-long sour stomach threatened a huge revenge. He was tanned and toned and handsome in a dark-haired, semi-effete way but his main flaw was his chin, which faded into his Adam's apple.

"Get over it." Krista glanced up from her text war to scold me.

I really needed to go for a run. "Aren't you the one who said puberty did him a solid by letting him grow a goatee, so we'd know where his face ended and his neck began?"

She shook her head, catching her bottom lip with her teeth. "You are hopeless."

"I don't care how much lipstick you slap on this pig, my dear, there's no way I'm going to get kissed." Because even if there was a likely suspect out there, he wouldn't be looking at me.

She jumped off her bunk and grabbed my arm. "Strap that dress on and let's get out of here, because it won't happen sitting in this cracker box."

In the end, I let her tie my dress and lend me some lipstick and even fix my hair in a semi-cute little up-do. Giving in was easier than fighting Hurricane Krista.

Chapter 4

"I feel naked," I murmured in Krista's general direction. She was half a step ahead of me on her way into the lodge's dining area.

She turned and glared over the top of her glasses, a look made even sterner by the hard line of her bangs. She'd taken out the ponytail and her straight dark hair fell to a precise finish just above her shoulders. "Ball up."

The sun-dress and hoodie combo hadn't bugged me during the ferry ride, and sitting at the edge of a conference room had been okay, but wearing something so far out of character in front of a group of professional acquaintances, coworkers, and friends made me want to hide under a trench coat. The cleavage had dropped at least two inches since we'd left the cabin, and without shorts I'd have no crotch protection if my skirt blew up.

"P. Kirk at ten o'clock," Krista said, *sotto voce*.

I locked my knees to keep from bolting. "What's the P stand for, anyway?"

"Performance." In her pink dress that looked like it was borrowed from a '60s housewife, Krista smirked and strutted off in the approximate direction of ten o'clock.

Rather than follow her, I glanced around the room for some other familiar faces. My fellow music teachers filled about half the seats in the dining hall, a huge room with windows looking out onto the beach and a bar in one corner. Each of the round tables could hold eight or ten people. The color scheme was built around watery greens and blues, with the kind of easy-to-clean, indestructible furniture found in places catering to the anonymous public.

The grade-school teachers had congregated in one corner so I headed in their direction, ignoring Krista's hiss. Predominately middle-aged and female, they were a safe group on which to try out my new look. I'd accrued several compliments and at least one person had asked where I shopped when something large and warm tapped on my shoulder.

I jerked around. "Yeah?"

Kirk Ringdahl handed me a glass of white wine. "Krista sent me over with this. You should come join us."

My jaw dropped open, though in the back of my mind I could hear Mom telling me to shut my mouth because I looked like a fish. "Sure."

His jovial smile forced his chin deeper into his neck, and though his hairline might have receded since the last retreat, he'd spent more time in the gym to compensate. And his smarmy attention implied I was some kind of prize. *Eek*.

While I was still floundering, he brushed my arm with his fingertips and led the way to his table. I followed, doing my best not to stumble on my sandals' tiny heels. Krista greeted me with a little round of silent, mission-accomplished applause.

Which wasn't obvious at all, except to anyone sitting at the table with two eyes and as many brain cells to rub together.

Kirk made an overproduction out of pulling me into the chair next to his, giving me yet another reason for embarrassment. Across the table, Jessica Freeman kept her beady hawk's eye on every move I made. She was a high school choir director, therefore closer to Kirk in social standing, and her vibe made it clear she did not appreciate my presence.

In addition to Jessica, four other members of P. Kirk's rooting section were taking me in with varying degrees of hostility. They all had good solid music-teacher names, like Jenny, Elaine, Karen, or Theresa. Except those weren't their actual names. I forgot them as soon as Kirk said them, and decided, at least in my own head, they were all named Sue. Old Sue, Not-As-Old Sue, Doesn't-Look-Old-Enough-For-College Sue, and Pregnant Sue were arrayed around Jessica like ladies-in-waiting. If she was the princess, then I was Cinderella's jock cousin.

And Krista was Loki and Anansi and Coyote all rolled into one.

"Maggie Schafer, Maggie Schafer, Maggie Schafer," Kirk drawled, his gaze traveling from my eyes to my mouth to parts further south. "I haven't seen you since the last time this fine group congregated."

I straightened my shoulders and cleared my throat. Just because I was dressed like a girl didn't mean I couldn't still kick his ass all over the softball field, and I'd be a born-again virgin before I gave it up to P. Kirk Ringdahl. He might be single and straight, but he was still a dweeb.

"Different schools, different school districts, you know." I funneled as much back-off-Jack into my voice as possible.

"If you had a seat on the council, we'd see each other at the meetings." He patted my hand and winked. "There's usually a chance for socializing after the business is done."

And I'd rather eat a rodent. "I'm pretty busy."

"I bet we could work something out."

Kirk fawned and Jessica sniffed and I had to sit on my hands to keep from popping him one. I gulped wine instead, then almost spewed it when Krista's pointy heel stabbed the top of my foot.

Amid a chorus of choking and laughter, one of the Sues tossed me a napkin and Krista managed to direct my attention to the doorway. My heart stilled. Stopped. Which was fine, because all the blood in my body rushed to my cheeks.

Except for the boiling puddle lower down.

All this because a certain Ginger God in faded jeans and a green T-shirt happened to be strolling into the room.

Chapter 5

While we'd been busy socializing, a buffet table had joined the bar, and servers began surreptitiously setting the tables for dinner. The room filled, the lights dimmed, and the smell of roasted garlic drowned out the old fish ocean smell. Kirk progressed from patting my hand to brushing my elbow to draping his arm in the general vicinity of my shoulders, and in self-defense, I went from clasping my hands to crossing my arms to sitting so straight I redefined perpendicular.

The man had an overdeveloped sense of his own animal magnetism, made worse by the presence of the Ginger God, who reduced Kirk's attractiveness to absolute zero.

The evening's guest speaker took the empty seat at our table. Professor Baumgartner had headed the music program at the University of Washington for years. His after-dinner talk would compare world music pedagogy with older methods of teaching. *Yawn.* He greeted each of us, then honed in on Jessica, whose girls' choir had received an honorable mention at State.

She glowed under his attention, giving me the chance to wonder why Kirk bothered with me when he could have someone like her. Her looks said sorority sister and Nordstrom shopper, while mine said too much softball. All the girly clothes in the world wouldn't hide the fact that I had the body of a muscular twelve-year-old boy.

Jessica punctuated each obsequious smile for the professor with a flirtatious smirk in Kirk's direction.

Or a pointed glare at me.

When the professor finished blowing smoke at Jessica, Pregnant Sue dragged me into the ring. "What about you, Maggie? Where do you teach?"

Too bad public school events couldn't serve hard liquor. I could have used a shot to take the sting away from her pseudo-friendly tone. "Lakewood Elementary."

"Oh, the littles? How cute." All the Sues sent up a chorus of squeals. "They're just so…enthusiastic."

"Yeah." And honest, and funny, and a whole lotta things grown-ups have forgotten how to be.

Servers lifted the tops off the hot dishes on the buffet line, and teachers from some of the other tables had started moving in the direction of food. Kirk put his hand over mine and leaned over in the direction of my ear, his voice low and throaty. "How come I never noticed you were so pretty?"

I stared at my fork and froze my smile in place. "I don't know."

"Maybe later we could go for a walk on the beach?"

Ick! "Ah, maybe. "

Professor Baumgartner stood and three of the Sues followed him, leaving me at the table with Jessica and Pregnant Sue. I scooted my chair away from the table, locked my fake grin in place, and prepared my escape.

"We haven't had much of a chance to talk," Kirk murmured, leaving a trail of slime in my ears.

"I just think elementary kids are a little dull, you know?" Jessica said to Pregnant Sue. They were facing each other, cutting us out of their conversation, while just as obviously talking loud enough for me to hear.

"What did you want to talk about?" I speared Krista with a glance, but she was forehead to forehead with one of the Sues. *Not the time for professional networking, BFF.* Unless she was over there planning my salvation, we were going to have words later.

Kirk ran his fingertips along the back of my neck. "I'm so happy you're here tonight."

Oh no. He did not just do that. I jumped out of my chair like it was time to make a break for home plate. "I'm going to get in line for dinner."

"Let's." He kept a hand on my elbow, guiding me toward the buffet line.

"I'm good." I jerked my arm away. "Really."

He seemed to take the hint—finally!—and we made it through the buffet line with a minimum of embarrassment.

Once everyone was seated, Kirk stood to give Professor Baumgartner an unnecessarily long introduction to the soundtrack of clanking silver and scraping plates. Most of the people in the room were UW graduates and already knew the professor, but we all smiled and applauded as Kirk spoke. He planted himself behind me, resting a hand on my shoulder, and after shifting in my seat, trying to shake it off, I gave up. Krista only shrugged and ignored me, like she thought a P. Kirk hookup was a done deal. Then I noticed the Ginger God seated at a table across from me.

Looking in my direction.

But not at my eyes.

He slouched in his chair, arms crossed as he gazed south of my shoulders, in the general direction of my breasts. My cheeks got warm and, even more embarrassing, my nipples got hard.

He smiled slowly, as if he noticed the last bit even from across the room, and his gaze traveled up even slower, peeling off my halter top on the way. His attention felt way too intimate for a room full of more than two hundred people. I shifted in my seat again, trying to ignore the burst of heat between my legs.

My independent streak started screaming about arrogance and invasion of privacy and inappropriate behavior. *Whatever.* My fingers twitched, ready to trace his Celtic tat and go exploring under his soft green T-shirt. For the first time in five years, three months, and five days, I wanted to be alone in a room with a man when he had that look in his eye.

Instead of listening to an illuminating debate on the possible applications of world music pedagogy compared with Dalcroze and Kodaly, I imagined how a Sex Diva would handle the situation.

And desperately wished the *Cosmo* article had some tips on cross-room eye sex.

The meal could well have been composed of sawdust and turpentine. The Ginger God's attention shifted when the servers started plunking dessert on the tables, leaving me chilled, like someone had just pulled the covers off me in bed. Krista was too absorbed in an exchange of text messages to talk, and Jessica and the Sues rose in a block. I followed close behind and made a break for the door.

Kirk caught me in the lobby, but as I was stumbling through some half-assed excuse about why I couldn't walk with him, a warm body pressed against my back and strong arms wrapped around my waist. Jerking my head to the side, I managed to plant my mouth on someone's waiting lips.

Warm. Soft. Tasting of savory man and smoke. I should have done something to escape, except he held me and turned me and pulled me closer. And kissing the Ginger God beat the high holy hell out of dealing with P. Kirk Ringdahl.

Chapter 6

Pretty much nothing in this life had prepared me for what to do when being held by one very attractive man while another one stood there sputtering. The crowd in the lobby might have quieted, or maybe I just couldn't hear them through the blood pounding in my ears. In the end, kissing the handsome stranger was much easier than dealing with everyone else's reaction.

And a lot more fun.

From some very distant place—or five feet away—Krista's little shriek pierced the cloud of steam surrounding my consciousness, and I eased away.

"Stay with me," the Ginger God whispered, and rested his chin on her head. "Sorry I was late, baby." He spoke for the whole room to hear. "My ferry got held up."

I did a quick series of calculations. I could introduce this guy to my backhand for being so bold, which would elevate the current situation from gossip-worthy to *OMG YOU WILL NOT BELIEVE WHAT I JUST SAW.*

I could play along, saving the lecture for later.

Or I could run like hell for the ferry.

It was only five miles or so.

Krista would bring my stuff home.

I snuggled closer to Ginger's chest. Couldn't run. Kitten heels. "Hey, Kirk."

The guy's voice rumbled through me and his woodsy scent pinged an internal reminder. *Duh.* I had a goal for this weekend.

"Randy." Kirk snapped the word like he wanted to jam it down the other man's throat.

Randy. The Ginger God had a name. I ran him through my mental database but didn't find a match. He wasn't an elementary music teacher, for sure. And Krista would have recognized him if he taught middle school. Maybe high school? East of the mountains? New in town?

"It's great to see you, man, but we were just leaving." With a two-fingered wave that started at his forehead and ended with finger guns, Randy tugged me toward the door.

I flashed a glance in Kirk's general direction. His face was red and his lips were tight and I considered moving *avoid Kirk Ringdahl* to my number-one goal for the weekend. But the heat in Randy's smile wouldn't let me change a thing.

Hand in hand, we strolled toward the cabins. The setting sun behind us stretched shadows across the gravel path.

"I hate guys like him," Randy said. He loosened his grip on my hand, but only so he could shift his position and put his arm around my shoulders.

I enjoyed the closeness, the heat from his body, his woodsy, male scent. "Good thing, because ol' P. Kirk'll carry a grudge."

"He can kiss my—"

Randy broke off with a laugh, so I patted the appropriate anatomic location. We reached the cabin I shared with Krista, but he kept us both moving onto the tiny porch of the cabin next door.

"We're neighbors," I said.

"Are we?" He faced me, still holding my hand. His green-eyed gaze was frank, honest, even through the shield of his glasses. "I'm Randy, by the way."

A shiver of excitement-need-desire shot through me. "And I'm Maggie."

"Well, Maggie, this was the most fun I've ever had with a music teacher."

His naughty grin sent another little lightning bolt deep in my belly. "Me too."

"Do you and Kirk have history?"

With a quick shrug, I loosened my shoulders and answered his question at the same time. "We do now."

He eased away to gaze out over the beach, bracing himself on the porch railing. I mirrored his movement. The tide was in, waves running along the baby sand dunes between the cabins and the water. The energy between us was companionable tinged with a buzz of attraction, and though I enjoyed the feeling, the beginnings of a problem disrupted my mood.

"Now there are two hundred music teachers who think we're here together," I said.

Randy rubbed a palm over his mouth in an unsuccessful attempt to hide a chuckle. "There were only about thirty in the lobby when I kissed you."

"Shut up." I batted at his arm. "By breakfast the whole group will have heard."

His laughter didn't dispute my claim. "Then we'll keep up the act. Why wouldn't they believe us? You're pretty." His gaze slid over me like warm lotion. "And I don't suck."

A hint of the predator I'd seen at dinner trapped me in his sight. I gulped and blushed and fought the urge to run. "So you'll protect me from Kirk, and I'll…what? What's in it for you?"

"I'll get the girl." He paused as if to let the promise, or threat, sink in. "We can keep it clean if you want," he added, though his tone suggested he'd prefer we didn't.

With a straight stare, I sized him up the way I would a pitcher on the mound. Was he throwing strikes, or trying to punk me? "Okay, it's a deal." Lifting my hand, I offered to shake.

"Hey, we're dating now. We're not going to shake on it."

He turned toward me, and as if by reflex I faced him.

"We're going to seal this deal with a kiss," he said.

"Sure." I rose on my toes and gave him a quick peck on the cheek, then swung my legs over the railing and hit the ground running before he could react.

Short skirt and kitten heels be damned.

Chapter 7

Krista crouched on her bunk, cell phone about four inches from her nose, thumbs flying. I slammed the cabin door and she tilted her face up, squinting to bring me into focus.

"You're not going to believe this." I whispered in case saying the words out loud would make things magically change.

Her thumbs slowed but didn't stop moving. "You accomplished your mission?"

I planted my fists on my hips and harrumphed at her.

"Just give me a minute. J-Bone wants to take the ferry over tomorrow afternoon so we can hang out tomorrow night, but I've already got plans with Troy."

She gave her full attention to her phone.

"Fine." Stomping past her to my own bunk, I finally, eagerly, gratefully, stripped out of the stupid halter dress. I stood there, naked except for my little thong panties, and dug through my bag for a T-shirt and pair of shorts. My bra stayed in the duffel bag, since my boobs weren't big enough to need the support. And so what if the shorts had started life as a pair of sweatpants until they'd met a pair of sharp scissors? No one but Krista would see them.

She'd have an opinion about them, of course. "Jesus, I liked it better when you were mooning me."

"That's enough out of you." I shook my finger at her like a crabby, scolding mother. "You got your way with the dress. Now it's my turn to be comfortable."

"Now it's your turn to spill. What the hell happened?"

"Randy kissed me." My giggle could have come from a hyperactive twelve-year-old. "And then we made a deal." I perched on the edge of my bunk, dismayed because the mattress wasn't any thicker than the palms of my hands. *People in the olden days must not have been into comfort.*

"I saw the kiss." Krista snickered right back at me. "Heck, I'm pretty sure there are pictures of you two floating around Facebook already."

"Really?" I covered my mouth in horror.

"No. Geez, chill out." She reached into her bag and pulled out the *Cosmo* magazine. "So this getting laid thing is a done deal, then. You've got it all set up."

"I'm set up for something." Grabbing the *Cosmo*, I flipped through to the sex diva article and gave Krista a recap of my conversation with Randy. She clapped her hands and smirked and hissed with so much excitement that by the end of my story I almost believed I'd be able to pull it off.

One of the article's sidebars caught my eye: *How To Sound Like a Dirty Diva. O-kay.* I tried to imagine telling Randy to put his big baby maker in my, um, my—

This was going to take some practice.

"So why are you hanging out in your unmentionables?" Krista snatched the magazine out of my hands. "You should be gettin' busy, you know, generating more gossip."

"No. More. Gossip." The coils wheezed when I flopped onto my skinny, antique mattress. "And by the way, what the hell did you say to Kirk that had him crawling all over me?"

She smirked into her fingertips. "Nothing."

I scanned the room for something heavy to throw at her. Nothing appropriate. Darn. "Someday there'll be payback, cutie pie."

"Talking tough, Maggie Jeanne, but you're the one with the agenda. I was just trying to help a friend in need."

"Stop calling me Maggie Jeanne." I plucked the magazine out of her hands. "Give me that. I need to study."

Her phone chirped and I was off the hook. She got involved in some arcane negotiation between men I'd never met, and I rehearsed naughty things to say to Randy. The article encouraged the kinds of thoughts I'd put away for the last few years, so there was the flood of deprivation to deal with. I got even hotter because I had a face to work with. A body to picture. A woodsy, smoky scent to recall.

At least until I started to worry he'd think I was too easy. In 2014, did women even care about doing the dirty deed with a guy they just met? Maybe I should have thought things through a little more before I made getting laid a goal for the weekend.

Falling asleep took quite a while.

The next morning, Krista and I sat cross-legged on the side of a dune, facing the water. The rising sun burned through the layer of light mist blurring the edges of the surrounding forest and the tide pulled out, leaving a lengthening stretch of damp sand between us and the water. The bagels were dry and the coffee came from a can, a severe offense for a Seattle brew snob. But I barely noticed. Anxiety and euphoria were dancing around in my belly like a pair of Japanese fighting fish. I might as well have been drinking seawater.

"So what happens next?" Krista asked.

"Don't know." Sand covered my toes and I nibbled on the bagel.

She belted my arm. "Wait, is that him?"

Gasping hard enough to inhale bagel crumbs, I got trapped by a spasm of coughing. When I could breathe again, I glanced off to the left. Randy stood near the edge of the water, his hands cupped in front of his mouth.

"What's he doing?" she whispered.

I wiped the tears out from under my eyelashes and shrugged. His hands dropped away and a puff of gray smoke swirled around his head.

"He just lit a cigarette."

She poked me hard in the ribs. "Go talk to him."

My heart raced faster than a shark chasing a minnow. A tasty minnow. A minnow decked out in the pretty new blouse her best friend insisted she buy. It only took a moment for my inner minnow to decide a Sex Diva wouldn't huddle on the beach, waiting for her handsome shark. I got up, kicked off my sandals, and strode across the cool sand.

I stopped a couple of feet from Randy, the edge of the sea splashing over the tops of my bare feet.

A subtle tilt of his head hinted that he heard me coming. Taking a final long drag on the cigarette, he put it out by dipping the tip in the water. "Most girls don't like the smell."

Between the light breeze and the rusty seaweed, I hadn't noticed. "Doesn't bug me."

"Yeah, you say that now." He faced me, moving an inch or so inside my personal space.

This close, his energy hummed against me, as if he'd run his hands over my skin without quite touching. I took a sip of coffee to cover the nerves pounding my gut in four-foot waves, then offered him the cup. "Want some?"

"Nah."

He moved another inch closer and lifted his hand. I froze, barely conscious of the cold water numbing my feet. He brushed a loose strand of hair out of my eyes, the edge of his fingernail gently scraping across my temple, and I shivered. "Why not?" I asked.

"Already had some." His brow creased, three parallel lines over his wire-framed glasses.

"Why do I want to kiss you so bad?"

I swallowed hard, my whole body vibrating. "You must be really getting into character."

"Yeah. Method acting." His smile was hot and naughty and gave me a peek at the tip of his tongue. "What have you got in your pocket?"

I rifled in the pockets of my brand-new jeans. "Maybe a price tag?"

He laughed at my confusion. "It's a method exercise. You're supposed to get to know your character so well, you can write down what they carry in their pockets."

"So—" I nibbled on a fingernail. "If my character is Randy's girlfriend, then I carry, what? An emergency pack of matches?"

"Right." He reached in fast to tickle my ribs. I giggled and blushed and smacked his hand away.

"We've got the rest of the weekend to figure out what goes where," he said. "Let's get through this morning's sessions, then we can go for a hike or something."

His *or something* fired up my pulse. "Sounds good."

"I mean, we're a couple, right? Everyone expects us to spend time together."

Swallowing down a sigh, I pasted on a watered-down version of his smile. "Sure."

Chapter 8

"So we start with a panel discussion, right?" Randy asked. His gray hoodie was unzipped far enough to show off the words "Baby Got Back" on his T-shirt.

"Yeah." Krista kicked at a tuft of beach grass. "Then there's a Boomwhackers workshop and some Orff instruments thing."

The three of us were close enough to the main lodge to be seen. Randy laced his fingers with mine as if he realized it was time to play a role. The excitement of flirting on the beach and introducing him to Krista faded a little. We were only faking it, after all.

Right?

As we walked across the lobby, little whispers rippled through the crowd of teachers the way waves are stirred up by the prow of a boat. I nudged Krista.

"Are people staring?"

I said it quiet enough only she should have been able to hear me, but Randy leaned over. "Yeah, they are, because the class fuck-up is hanging out with the prettiest girl here."

His lips brushed my ear, which set off a delicate flurry of sensation. Like tickles, but hotter. I flinched, grinned, rubbed my cheek against my shoulder. Randy laughed into my hair. By the time I could pull sentences together, we'd moved on. I made a note to ask him what he meant. Later. When we were no longer the center of attention. From what I could tell he wasn't a fuck-up, and for sure I wasn't the prettiest girl here.

In the main conference room, rows of long tables had been set up. Water glasses and pitchers had been set at intervals, with a podium and microphone off in one corner. Kirk stood behind the podium, laughing with one of the Sues. Krista wanted to claim a front table, to make it easier for everyone to stare, and I insisted we sit in the last row. In the end, we compromised on seats in the middle of the room.

Sitting between Randy and Krista was like sinking into the safety of a shadow, and my new perspective showed me the whole room wasn't, in fact, watching us. People only paid attention to their own stuff. Likely my own self-consciousness made me feel like the main attraction. Kirk scanned the room, his gaze passing over our seats, then looping back around.

So maybe a few people were watching us.

Kirk's amplified throat-clearing brought the crowd to order. "Good morning." His smile put an exclamation point on his words. "Before we break out into our age-specific workshops, the planning committee and I thought it would be fun to have the whole group brainstorm ideas for how to increase student engagement."

"For once we might talk about the important stuff, like how to get sixth-grade boys to sing," Krista muttered into her fist.

"In a moment I'm going to introduce our moderator," Kirk continued, oblivious to Krista's editorial comment, "who will lead us in a discussion of strategies you've used successfully."

"Like how to keep the kindergartners from peeing on the carpet," I said, covering my comment by pretending to adjust the drawstring neckline of my blouse. Randy noticed and gave the laces a gentle tug, bringing the fabric about three millimeters lower. When he patted my hand as if to say "good girl," I kicked him in the shin.

He snickered.

So did Krista, though for a different reason. "Pee on the carpets? That's *so* why I teach middle school."

"Yeah. You'd rather catch your students making out in the instrument room."

Krista's giggle had heads turning, and I had to bite on a knuckle to keep from making any noise. Apparently oblivious to us, Kirk introduced the moderator, Bailey. She was a motivational speaker, one of those super-trim, super-polished, permanently attractive older women who had probably been a *Cosmo* subscriber since she graduated from college. To wake us up, she had us stand and give each other neck massages. Randy's hands felt strong and warm and sure on my neck, though when it was my turn to massage him, I spent as much time trying to work his collar low enough to reveal more tattoos as I did working the muscles of his neck and shoulders.

When we were all seated again, Bailey grabbed the mic. "So we're here to talk about engagement." She stalked across the front of the room on her tailored four-inch heels. "What it means. How it works. Your kids' engagement. Your engagement."

My engagement? My head knew she was using a '90s buzz-word. My heart didn't want to talk about it.

"I checked out the word on Dictionary.com," Bailey continued. "Among other things, it means 'to occupy oneself; to take employment; to pledge one's word, and assume an obligation.'"

She paused, allowing the word "obligation" to filter into our consciousness. I reached over and poured myself some water from the pitcher on our table. Anything to distract me from the direction my thoughts had taken. Bailey kept talking, and I kept thinking. Had Creighton and I felt an obligation toward each other? We'd been twenty-three and twenty-five years old when we got engaged. With the benefit of a few years' distance, the glaring contrast between how mature I'd felt compared with how young and idiotic I'd been stood out like neon at midnight. I could also ask myself a few hard questions. Like, had I really loved him, or had I just been terrified at being on my own? If he'd been able to walk away from our pledge so easily, had it ever meant anything?

Randy shifted his weight, pressing his knee against the side of mine and curling his fingers around my shoulder. Why was I thinking about the bad old days now? I rested my hand on Randy's thigh, fighting the urge to dig in. His heat made my palm itch. With desire.

I lost track of Bailey's discourse, at least until she threw things open for discussion. Someone asked the group whether using rap music in the classroom was a good idea, and I raised my hand. After a minute, the moderator brought me the mic. She tried to get me to stand up, but I spoke from the safety of my seat. "Meeting the kids on their level is the most important thing."

"So do you use rap music in the classroom?" she asked.

"Sometimes. It depends on the lyrics and the age of the kids." I smiled into the room, avoiding everyone's gaze. "I've used One Direction, Lady Gaga, even Macklemore with the older kids. Heck, my students love Albannach, the Scottish drum band."

"I do think it's a problem, though, when kids get to high school with a better understanding of *American Idol* than they do of music theory." Jessica Freeman projected her trained performer's voice from across the room without even waiting for the mic. I caught a few of the daggers she was throwing with her eyes and handed the mic to Bailey. She took a couple of quick steps in Jessica's direction.

"But I guess they know how to polka, so there's that." After delivering her parting shot, Jessica resumed her seat.

Hopefully the lump of embarrassment in my belly would be heavy enough to pull me through the floor. In case it didn't, I retreated between Krista and Randy, sure I was the only one who thought Jessica acted like a—

"Bitch," Randy whispered, shifting restlessly beside me.

Krista used stronger language.

"Before we wrap this up, I wonder if anyone could speak to how to handle things if your high school kids have addiction issues." Kirk surveyed the room, microphone in hand. "Is Randy still here? Randy Devers?"

Kirk smiled so hard in our direction, his chin all but disappeared. "I'm sure you could share some great hands-on experience."

Randy tensed but didn't move his arm from around me. "I don't know, Kirk. I think you treat an addict like anybody else." He paused, the scuff of Bailey's heels on the rug the only noise in the room. Randy started speaking again before she could get him the mic. "Most kids who are in recovery have education plans, so we're working in the context of the educational team."

"Right on. It's a team effort."

I had no idea what was going on, but Randy's normal confidence was underlined by strain, and I wanted to take Kirk's jovial smirk and shove it up his ass.

Someone jumped in with a question about teamwork, and Bailey played the moderator card, moving the conversation in a different direction. I caught Krista with her elbow on the table and her cheek on her fist, giving Randy a look that was one part speculation and three parts sympathy.

Clearly my acting partner kept more in his pocket than his pack of Winston Lights.

When Bailey dismissed us, Randy was one of the first people out the door. I followed, every one of my protective instincts firing. Which was totally crazy, since I'd only known him for a day.

Talk about your easy engagements.

Chapter 9

I caught up with Randy on the beach. He stood with his back to the lodge, his arms crossed, giving the water a sardonic smile. Krista bleated at me from the path to the cabins. I ignored her.

I crossed the line where the stones and broken shells gave way to smooth sand. Randy must have heard me, but he didn't move. My first impulse was to wrap my arms around him. Could be an invasion of his privacy. Could really piss him off. Could be what he'd expect of a girlfriend.

My hands overlapped on his belly and I pressed my forehead in the warm hollow between his shoulders and his neck. He stiffened, inhaled, relaxed.

"Dude's a dick," he said.

I flattened my palms over his ribs. I didn't know what to say, so I kept quiet and held him close. His ginger curls brushed across my brow and I burrowed deeper into his musky, smoky scent.

He covered my hands with one of his and stuffed his cigarettes in the back pocket of his jeans, bumping my lower belly with his knuckles. "We should go to the break-out sessions."

"In a minute," I murmured against him.

"If I'm late they'll just have more to bitch about." He squeezed my wrist and stepped away. "Let's go."

Guess I'd overreacted. I dodged his eyes with a quick inspection of the ocean. "Okay. Yeah." We barely knew each other. "Let's go."

Because I wasn't, in fact, his girlfriend.

I'd made it about four steps when he bumped into me. "Thanks."

"For what?" Our hands tangled and our feet tangled and I almost stumbled.

"For keeping up the act."

Oh yeah. We hadn't just shared a moment. We were ACTING, in capital letters. I had no right to the squishy, warm feelings burbling around inside.

"Hey, we've got some time between the break-out sessions and the concert this afternoon." He tugged on my sleeve, playfully pulling it a little further off my shoulder. "Still wanna go hike?"

"Oh my God, how awesome." I hadn't had a decent run since before the softball game on Thursday. I needed an exercise fix worse than any junkie. A good hard hike would help me manage the emotional overload.

We hit the lobby and he planted a quick kiss on my temple. "Go play with your Orff instruments and I'll see you in a while."

"Sure."

He didn't see my half-assed wave.

I ducked into the first grade-school-appropriate workshop I came to. Fortunately I didn't know any of the participants, so no one asked me how long I'd been dating the hot redhead.

Not sure how I would have answered their questions.

Two hours later I was on the front porch of my cabin. I'd draped my peasant blouse over a chair so it wouldn't wrinkle and changed into a pair of cropped khaki pants and an orange tank top with a plaid shirt open over top of it. I had my Merrill boots and a water bottle and if Randy didn't show up in about ninety seconds I was heading out without him.

He came jogging along the path with only seconds to spare. "Nice pigtails," he said, raising his eyebrows at my hairstyle on his way into his cabin.

A minute later he came out. He'd changed out of his jeans into a pair of shorts, and he had a water bottle in one hand. "On my way in yesterday I passed a trailhead about a quarter mile away."

"Let's go."

Side by side, we headed for the main road, settling into an easy pace and a companionable silence. Except for the way my skin tingled whenever he accidentally brushed against me, things were good. And when my skin tingled, things were great. I couldn't help but notice the firm curve of his butt and the reddish gold hairs covering his muscular calves.

I busted him checking me out, too.

"So you really make your kids listen to Scottish pipes?" he asked.

"Shut up. They love Albannach." I laughed, warming up, muscles loosening. We reached the trailhead and the promise of shade under the pine forest.

"This might be dumb," I said, "but I don't even know where you teach."

"Parkridge High." He paused at the entrance to the trail and took a deep breath. "Fucking smokes."

I let one raised eyebrow voice my opinion.

"I've been the band director there for the last couple of years, and Chelsea McMillan's got the choirs." He started walking, waving me on with a shamefaced grin. "The principal wanted one of us here, but she's on medical leave." Another guilty smile. "Douchebags like Kirk piss me off so bad I usually steer clear of this scene."

Aha! So that was why I'd never seen him at these things before. "I'm not sure how Krista talked me into going."

"It's better than torturing children with bagpipes."

"Hush, you, or I'll make you walk faster."

Laughter laced his wheezy cough. "All right. I'll behave."

The trail curved up the side of a ridge in a series of lazy switchbacks. Big cedars and fir trees surrounded us, their energy dampening our voices and silencing our footsteps. When we reached a clearing, we stopped for a breather. On one side, the ground dropped several hundred yards to the rocky shoreline. I slipped off my pack, shivering a little when the breeze hit the sweaty patches between my shoulder blades.

Randy reached for a cigarette.

"Seriously? Dude, some forest Nazi's going to shoot you." My schoolteacher's voice got the better of me as I scolded him.

"Just a couple of puffs and I'll put it out." With a soft scratch he struck a match, but turned away as if he was ashamed for me to watch him light up. "You're not the only one who gives me shit about it."

"And I'm probably not the only one who tells you to quit, then."

The end of the smoke crackled on his inhale. "My girls lecture me daily."

Girls? Daily? What? I must have been giving him my open-mouthed fish stare again, because he started talking before I responded.

"I think you're the only one here who doesn't know." He stuffed the pack away with a shake of his head. "Sky Valley High class of 2000. Won the Quincy Jones award for best jazz player in the state. Had a full ride to Berklee in Boston, and the only things I cared about were my horn, my girl Mary Pat, and getting high."

He paused, as if he wanted to let his words sink in. "One night a month before school started, MP and I tore it up. We were so lit I wrapped the passenger side of my car around a light pole. I stood trial for vehicular assault and driving under the influence. She's a paraplegic."

Hadn't seen that one coming. I made a sound somewhere between sympathy and a prompt, finding a salmonberry shrub to examine so he wouldn't see me blinking through the tears.

"So yeah, needless to say, I didn't go to Berklee. My parents got me into rehab, and now I teach high school kids to play instead of being the big session guy in New York." Our eyes met. His gaze was guarded, uncertain, as if my reaction mattered.

A mix of sadness and anger roiled my gut. Damn that P. Kirk Asshole for taunting a guy who'd been through so much. I used the anger to lock down my expression, because tears would embarrass us both. "I'm sorry."

He relaxed and reached for my hand. Regardless of whatever else happened, this moment was *not* an act.

"It took MP less time to forgive me than it did for me to forgive myself." His words were aimed at the dirt, like we were pushing his limits for sharing.

"Do you keep in touch with her?"

He twined his fingers through mine. "Yeah. She and her girlfriend live about a mile from me."

"Um ..."

"You know, so they can harass me about smoking." Stroking the back of my hand with his thumb, he tugged me closer to his body. "We're better friends than we were lovers."

His chuckle gave me permission to exhale.

"They've got two kids now, which keeps them out of my hair."

"For sure."

After another long drag, he stubbed out the cigarette.

"Seems like it'd mess with your wind."

"Try playing trumpet." His hoarse cackle illustrated the point.

"Nah, I'll stick to my harp, thanks." I uncapped my water bottle, like I was going to use it to douse the growing intensity between us. "You play anything besides trumpet?"

"Sure do." He took a step closer, then another, his moves as sleek as the opening gesture of a tango. "They say kissing a smoker is like licking an ashtray."

So much for self-disclosure. I shied away, arms across my chest, not quite ready to dance. "Wow, sounds appealing."

"You already had a taste." He shadowed my movements, his voice a sexy rumble. "Maybe you'll want to try it again."

"Maybe." Like sometime between now and when we all had to go home.

"Let's hang out here for a while." He pulled me over to a sunny stretch of grass.

Maybe I'd find out about kissing an ashtray a lot sooner than I expected.

Chapter 10

The hush around us thickened, as if the trees were watching to see what we'd do next. We sat cross-legged in the grass, surrounded by a low pulse that either came from the ocean below us or possibly from the crazy pounding of my own heart. Randy's glasses did little to filter the intensity in his gaze, and I reached out, touching his arm where the bottom edge of his tattoo showed beneath his sleeve. "Is this your only tat?"

The heat in his grin doubled the speed of the low pulsing sound. "Um, no."

My hand fell to my side as I opened and closed my mouth, trying for a snappy comeback. Something in my belly was having a little conniption fit. Krista said I should try something new, and *Cosmo* told me a Sex Diva should be BOLD, be CONFIDENT, be DIRECT. I didn't always follow others' advice, but this seemed like a *carpe diem* kind of moment.

I swallowed hard before I spoke. "Can I see them?"

"What?"

"Your tattoos."

The predator returned full strength, and my breath caught on the inhale.

"Some of them," he said.

A couple of birds zipped across the path behind us, chasing each other through the trees. Randy slowly pulled his shirt off and stretched out in the grass, resting on his elbows. The vine around his upper arm became a powerful dragon and wrapped over his shoulder, its claws holding some kind of knot-work symbol over his heart. My finger traced the pattern in the vine before my brain identified the movement. His skin was soft, warm, and when I added a second finger, he exhaled heavily through his nose.

I breathed faster, mouth open. Tried to moisten my lips with the tip of my tongue. Froze in the heat of his predator's gaze.

"It's not fair," he said. "I'm half naked, and you're not."

He had a point. I shrugged out of my plaid shirt. My hiking shorts were not really Sex Diva wear, but his eyes were fixed on where sweat had stuck my thin tank top to my chest. I rose onto my knees. He stretched further till he was almost lying in the grass. My skin was moist all over, and not just from the hike.

No acting class anytime, anywhere ever taught anyone how to deal with the palpable energy between us. His smile said *come and get it*, and since we weren't playing by the rules, I did.

I leaned forward, tensed every muscle for control, and kissed the knot over his heart, making the gesture as delicate as possible. Teasing us both. I planted a hand on either side of his chest. Bold. Confident. Direct.

Melting.

"What's it mean?" I shifted to lay a fingertip on the symbol I'd just kissed.

He shrugged. "Strength. Power." He tipped his head up, giving himself a double chin to see where I was pointing. "I fought the dragon and won."

I crawled over him. He stretched, slow and supple, the way a cat does after it's been asleep for a while, and ended up with his head resting in his hands and his elbows spread wide. "Are you going to kiss me or not?" he asked.

"You're all laid out like some kind of steamy sexy banquet."

He chuckled from deep in his belly. "I could say 'eat me,' but that would be a pretty painful joke."

I bent lower, laughing, getting as close to his lips as I could. Rather than kiss him, I stuck out my tongue and licked.

I mean, a Sex Diva might be bold and all, but teasing was good, too. With a sudden move, he tipped me onto my ass. He got an arm around me and rolled, and before I caught my breath he was the one on top. "Now," he said, almost a snarl, "are you going to kiss me or not?"

Rubbing my knuckles across the scruff of beard on his chin, I caught the hinge of his glasses and pulled them off. "Sure."

Our kiss in the lobby had been playful, as if both of us were surprised to find ourselves lip to lip.

This one was serious.

Randy moved in, all pro-skilled lady-killer confidence, but when our mouths touched, we both got real. His kiss had heat, and fight, and sweetness, and when he moved away, his brows were drawn like he couldn't quite believe what we'd done. When he moved toward me a second time, my mouth opened and I flicked his bottom lip with my tongue.

That did it.

Striking fast, he locked his lips on mine, crushing me under his body. We made out like high schoolers, stretched out in the grass and bathed in sunshine. Yeah, he tasted a little like cigarettes, but when he held my face with both hands and destroyed me with his lips and tongue, I all but melted. I covered his hands with mine, twining my tongue in his, grinning a little at the rough burn of his beard against my chin. Underneath the cigarettes I tasted Man, and loved the reminder of how good it could be.

He shifted his weight and I rubbed my thigh against his hardness, which set off a flaming bottle rocket in my belly. My feminine bits were buzzing with need and my hands were free to roam and I reveled in the way his muscles tensed under my touch.

Five years of pent-up emotion threatened to come barreling through. I broke the kiss, breathing hard. His unfocussed expression amazed me, as if the passion riding me had grabbed him just as hard.

Voices from the trail broke open our mood. Randy's eyes narrowed. Both of us stiffened. He groaned and rested his forehead on my collarbone.

"We should get to the outlook in another mile," P. Kirk Ringdahl said, echoed by a choir of Sues. Because of course Kirk should wander by. Obviously.

"Doesn't he have a class to teach or something?" I whispered. "Or somebody else's day to ruin?"

Randy didn't move, and I didn't move, and after a while the voices faded.

"I don't think they saw us," I said, though my visual field was limited to the trees overhead and a certain dragon tattoo.

"Doesn't matter." Randy sat up, mouth tight. He grabbed for his glasses and shoved them on. "We should probably get back."

More than a little confused by where the act ended and his true interest began, I reached for my blouse. "Okay, yeah."

On our way back to the cabins, the birds made more noise than we did. Randy left me at my door, saying he'd see me at the concert. I had a whole lot of curdled naughty to deal with, and decided I'd shower and go find Krista. She'd either straighten me out or confuse things further, but at least she'd listen.

Chapter 11

Krista used a damp towel to wipe the steam off the tiny bathroom mirror. "With that kind of history, no wonder the guy's a little flaky."

"Right? Every time I think he might actually like me, something happens and we start play-acting again." I tightened the second towel under my armpits and went out into the cabin's stuffy main room. We had the door shut and the curtains drawn so we could walk around undressed without giving all the other music teachers a show.

Krista stepped into the room, tying the belt of her cute little vintage kimono wrap. "So? I mean, this isn't a long-term deal anyway, right? Get laid and get out."

I bent to dig through my duffel bag and the towel dropped to the floor. Frustrated, I just let it lie there. "It's like the only reason he's doing this is to jerk Kirk around."

"Again, so? After tomorrow you never have to see him again."

Somehow the thought made me a little nauseated. Randy had an appealing, grown-up kind of confidence, like he'd seen enough of life to separate the wheat from the bullshit, and the more time I spent with him, the more time I wanted to.

I dropped onto my bunk, hands resting between my knees. We were supposed to go watch three award-winning choirs perform, one from each age range, and while I normally loved to hear kids sing, my fountain of enthusiasm had turned into a murky puddle.

"Aw, don't listen to me if it's going to make you droopy. You know I'm only good at the fun part." Krista eased into the bathroom. "If a guy starts to have actual feelings, I'm gone."

I stood and slowly brought my clasped hands behind my neck, arching my lumbar spine into the stretch. I let my head drop forward and used my wrists to give it an extra pull. Krista was right about one thing. I needed to get laid, and get out.

"Geez, I never knew you were such a nudist. Go put on something cute," Krista called from the bathroom.

I grabbed a pair of yoga pants from my bag, along with a stretch lace top. As a concession, I slipped into the pair of kitten-heel sandals from Target. I pulled my hair into a short ponytail and put on a gold chain necklace and small hoop earrings. The teachers, and Krista, and Randy, were going to have to live with my choices.

She popped out of the bathroom wearing a pair of pedal-pusher jeans and a blouse with the collar turned up. Since we were both decent, I opened the door and the curtains. A little breeze came off the water, replacing the musty cabin air with salt. Krista's makeup ritual was more elaborate than mine, so I had time to kill. I sat cross-legged on my bunk and reached for the *Cosmo* magazine. It naturally opened to the pertinent article.

"Stupid J-Bone said his plans had changed *again*, and now he can meet us out in Langley tomorrow." Krista leaned into the mirror, mascara brush in hand. "But when he canceled I made plans with Robbie." The brush slipped. "Shit." She turned to me, wiping away a smudge with the tip of her finger. "So now I can't decide if I should tell one of them not to come, and if so, which one. Or maybe I should bag on both of them and take my chances meeting somebody new."

I loved Krista like a sister, but her rotating cast of male companions exhausted me. "Maybe we should just go hear the band play and let nature take its course."

"We're going to go hear a band play? Where?" A male voice from the doorway startled me. Randy stood right outside. He knocked against the door frame a couple of times and grinned at me. I folded the magazine and shoved it under the pillow, my cheeks way hotter than they needed to be.

"Langley. Tomorrow night." Krista raised her chin and stroked her mascara, a teensy smirk the only evidence of her intent to cause trouble.

"I thought the conference ended tomorrow afternoon," he said.

"It does." I stood, half thinking of greeting him with a quick kiss. Actually, I had to stand because really I had an overwhelming visual of what kind of tattoo he might have at the end of his treasure trail and sitting on a bed seemed like a really bad idea.

Damned Cosmo.

"We're staying an extra night so we can hear the Blues Revivalists play over in Langley." I didn't do any kissing and squashed the visualizing as best I could. "You should come with us."

Did I really just ask a guy out?

His grin softened. "That'd be cool." It took him three steps to invade my personal space, and when he got there, he ran a fingertip down the side of my cheek.

I smiled despite myself. Turning into his hand was just too easy.

"Are you staying here the extra night?" he asked.

I shook my head, brushing his knuckles with my lips. This—whatever it was—between us wasn't going to last, but temporary didn't mean I had to give up on right now. "We've got a reservation in Langley."

He cupped my cheek with his palm. "Might be too late to get one myself. Can I crash with you?"

The elevator dropped out from under my tummy. "Sure."

"Get a room," Krista intoned. She came through the door and tossed her makeup bag in her suitcase. "C'mon, lovers. It's time to go admire Jessica Freeman's fabulous fillies."

Randy bumped my forehead with his and I moaned. Kids choirs were *so* not where I wanted to be. With just a little more prodding from Krista, we all headed over to the lodge.

Chapter 12

The best part about the concert was sitting next to Randy, and the best part about dinner was my anticipation of dessert.

And I'm not talking ice cream.

Actually, the dinnertime entertainment wasn't bad, either. While working on our leathery lasagna, we were treated to the Kirk and Jessica Show, which involved fawning and giggling and at least one masculine sigh. The whole production got an under-the-table round of applause. For his big finish Kirk kissed her right in front of the fruit punch.

"He has all the technique of a mother bird delivering a worm to her chicks," Krista said in my ear. I had to walk out of the dining hall to keep from embarrassing myself.

After dinner, Krista borrowed my car keys and took off. She'd renegotiated things with Robbie and was meeting him in Langley for some unspecified activity I really didn't want to know too much about. Which left me and Randy.

Standing between our two cabins.

Where the setting sun was turning the ocean from aqua to navy to indigo.

Holding hands.

"So…goodnight?" he said.

Disappointment nailed me. "I should go in and do some reading." *Because Sex Divas so often spend the night alone with a good book.*

"Me too."

Neither of us moved.

Time for me to be bold. Confident. Direct. And maybe try a compliment. According to the fine folks at *Cosmo*, *A Little Sugar Goes a Long Way.*

"Guess what. I lied." I faced him, which was an awkward choice because the faded amber light reflected off his glasses, hiding his eyes. "I don't have a book to read. I was kind of …" I tugged gently on his shirt, right above where it tucked into his jeans. "Hoping you'd show me …" Nerves temporary disabled my ability to speak. I cleared my throat and pressed on. "Your tattoo is so amazing, and you said you had others."

He wrapped his hands around my waist and drew me closer to his body. "I don't show them off to just every girl."

Though I couldn't read his eyes, his firm hold and his half smile and the little gap between his lips told me he liked where I was headed. I slid my fingers into the front pockets of his jeans. "Can we go to your cabin? In case Krista and Robbie have a fight and she has to crash here."

His smile broadened, but he didn't give me an answer. The pause lasted long enough to make my heart stumble. Maybe I'd misjudged the situation, totally misinterpreted the cocoon of tension and heat wrapped around us whenever we were alone. All right, no. I'm not an idiot. The zoom-y sensations were real. There had to be some reason he was holding me off. I took a deep breath, struggling to say something lame to get us both off the hook.

And then I held that breath, because his lips locked onto mine like I was a fountain and he was a thirsty, thirsty man. Holding me in place with a hand to the back of my head, he caught me in a torrent of fierce kisses, tearing at my lips, drowning me in sensation. I gasped, which gave him an opening, and his tongue found mine. I tasted smoke and promise and savory man, and I returned his energy with a dividend, cascades of pent-up emotion surging through the connection between us.

When he finally broke the kiss, I sagged against him, my belly pressed against his, his hardness rubbing my thigh. "Your cabin, then?" It took me a couple of tries to get the words out, and when they came, my voice was a haggard whisper.

He didn't even bother answering, just clutched my hand and dragged me along the path. We stopped on his front porch.

"How come you don't have a roommate?" I asked, nerves making me pick at details.

Randy fumbled with the key for a moment, then pushed open the creaky old door. "The guy from Roosevelt canceled."

He kicked off his shoes before going in, so I followed suit. Then we were inside, facing each other in the dusky twilight and saltwater air. His cabin had a dresser against the wall at the foot of one of the bunks and a small table under the window. We both sat, as if now that things were getting serious we needed a break before taking the plunge.

"I've got some sodas in the cooler," he said.

"Could really use a shot." I spoke mostly to myself, then pressed my palms together in front of my mouth when I remembered why he'd offered soda instead of something stronger.

Resting his palms on the table, he gave me a rueful shrug. "Nope."

I covered his hands with my own. "Guess you'll just have to deal with my nerves, then."

Rueful gave way to naughty, and he flipped his hands over to grasp mine. He only let go long enough to slide his glasses off and toss them on the table. He looked younger without them, stronger, as if he could see deeper without his wire-framed shield.

"So you know my sordid story," he said. The only other sound was the steady wash of the waves running over the beach. "What's yours? You're too pretty to be single." He coughed a little after he spoke, clearing smoke out of his lungs.

I coughed, too, or rather choked. *Too pretty to be single? Right.* "Creighton Kleig."

"Kleig? The piano guy?"

"Yeah, you know him?"

Randy shrugged. "I did a few gigs with him, before he left for L.A. He's kind of an asshole."

"We were engaged." I let the thought peter out.

He rubbed a knuckle through the shadow of a beard on his chin. "Didn't he, like, dump some girl at the altar?"

"Well, technically I hadn't left the hair salon, but close enough."

"You?" He squeezed my hand and looked me full in the face.

I could only meet his gaze for a second before I had to pull away. This was the big scary black hole I'd let dominate my life for the past five years, four months, and I'd lost track of how many days. I swallowed hard and squared my shoulders. "Cost my Dad a crap-ton of money."

"Shit." He drummed a finger on the table. "Well, shit."

"I have some trust issues." I hoped the cliché would help us laugh it off.

Neither of us even chuckled.

"Well," he spoke on a sigh, "if dealing with MP and Vaughan has taught me nothing else, it's that if I say I'm going to do something, I do it."

Saying the words out loud made the hole smaller somehow, shrunk it, made it less dramatic and more of a manageable sadness. I laughed, breathing deep, surrounded by the combination of sea air and cigarettes I'd come to associate with Randy. "How is it you're still single? Guys who call when they say they will are rare."

"And girls who don't freak out when a guy tells her he went through recovery and has kids with a lesbian couple are also rare."

"Yeah, well…wait." I jerked on his arm, using it to leverage myself to standing. "You didn't tell me they were your kids."

I closed the distance between us, and he shifted around so I could plant myself between his knees. It was a toss-up which of us had the naughtier grin.

He put his hands on my butt, holding me in place. "Is that a deal-breaker?" His steady massage stirred up all kinds of heat. "Because jacking off on a gurney behind a curtain in a clinic, well, it's not the same as…"

As what? All of a sudden I couldn't think of much besides the more conventional way to make babies, and the way he kept stroking my ass made it pretty plain his mind had headed in a similar direction. A tiny thread of excitement got caught in my throat.

This was *it.*

Chapter 13

Though I'd only known Randy for a day or so, I'd been waiting a good long time to get to this moment. Sitting in his little cabin, his eyes as dark as the forest at night, the tension vibrating from him resonated with the mix of fear and excitement dancing through me. The regular rhythm of the waves gave us a soundtrack, and for a long moment we paused, taking each other in.

Then he stood, wrapping his arms around me and crushing me against his body. He paused with his lips so close the warmth of his breath brushed over me, and then he dove in. This was no tentative will-he-or-won't-he press on my lips. No, the hunger in me roared from deep in my belly, heated by parts of my anatomy even further south. It knocked us both sideways, landing us on the bunk.

Randy squinted, as if he couldn't quite bring me into focus without his glasses. He lay beneath me, stretched full out and apparently enjoying his fuzzy view. "You're making it hard to keep my pants on," he said.

I quieted him with another kiss, playing with his lips, nipping at the corner of his mouth. His hands slipped under my shirt and molded to my back.

"No bra," he said, the words more of a gasp against my neck.

I just smiled and worked my legs in between his, pressing my belly against his hard length and continuing an onslaught of kisses. I wanted him, plain and simple. The retreat, Kirk, his past and mine all faded, softer than the sound of the waves out on the beach. My inner Sex Diva came out and I didn't even try to fight her.

It was time to make something new.

"You're a good kisser," I said, easing away so I could meet his gaze.

He smiled, a look both mocking and amused. "Horn player."

"And your good hands?" I gasped as he tweaked my nipple.

"Piano." He shifted his weight, pushing our groins together and leaving no doubt as to what his little head wanted. "Let me see you," he whispered, reaching for the hem of my stretchy top.

He pulled it off over my head and his low whistle told me all I needed to know. He rolled us both to the side, one arm under my shoulders and the other hand doing amazing things to my breasts. This time his kiss had more intention, his tongue thrusting, both of us panting. I scooted his shirt up as far as I could and we broke the kiss so he could pull it off over his head.

We lay pressed together, my nipples tingling where they rubbed against the ginger hairs on his chest. He ran lazy kisses over my chin and down my neck. "Are we having sex or not?" he asked, his lips moving just above the base of my throat.

I curled my upper body so I could whisper into his ear. "Do you have a condom?"

He dropped onto his back, laughing. "One."

I shifted, curving myself along the side of his body and fighting a squeal of excitement because we were talking about having sex. My heart beat faster than any Irish reel, and the slippery heat between my legs needed Randy's attention. Badly.

Trailing gentle circles through the hair on his chest, my fingers stopped at his belt buckle. "You weren't a Boy Scout, I guess."

"Hell, yes. That's why I carry one. I just didn't figure this weekend would put a big demand on my supply."

"But you thought you might need one?" I went to work loosening the buckle of his belt.

He pulled me down for a kiss. "Be prepared."

A brand-new box of condoms was hidden in the bottom of my bag, but if I ran over to my cabin, would I lose my nerve completely? *Hmm.* According to the *Cosmo* article, I needed to find a frenulum to flick. We could deal with the issue of prophylactics later.

"Come here," I whispered, then slid to the floor on my knees.

Eyes narrowed in a thoughtful skepticism, he swung his legs to the floor in front of me, close enough to run my fingertips along his belly. I pulled the band out of my hair and shook it loose, then scooted over, inviting him to stand. Using my shoulder for leverage, he did, and I went work on his jeans, button after frustrating button. He *would* wear vintage Levi's. I dragged his pants over his butt, feeling around for his nonexistent boxers.

Oh. Commando.

He chuckled, the sexiest sound ever, and scuffed his jeans off the rest of the way. "What are you up to?"

"Shh." I lay a fingertip on my lips. His wicked smile gave me all kinds of encouragement, but still I paused, eye level to one of the most beautiful things I'd ever seen.

A band matching the one on Randy's upper arm had been tattooed just above his right knee. A trailing vine rose from it, wrapping around his thigh and creeping up. The vine became a serpent, climbing over his hip and ending just above his pubic bone. I couldn't actually see the serpent's head through his erection, but made a leap of logic from my position on the floor.

I traced my fingers along the tattoo, the motion punctuated by his sharp intake of breath. Leaning forward, I pressed my face against him, nuzzling the coarse curls at the base of his shaft, breathing in the musky masculine smell that had nothing to do with cigarettes or salt water.

I cupped his balls with one hand and grasped the base of him with the other. His muttered "shit" sent a buzz of excitement to my happy place. Good. He liked my idea. I needed this, needed him, needed to be in charge of how I got new memories.

"You put your mouth on me," he said, drawing in a quick breath as I ran my fingertips along his shaft, "and we're pretty much going to be having sex."

"Yeah." I turned the word into a soft whistle, blowing over the head. He pulsed in my grip, and after culling the memories of the *Cosmo* article for a few more ideas, I took him in my mouth.

The last time I'd given a blow job, I was so scared I'd do something wrong, neither of us had much fun. This time I let the sounds he made and the shivery tension in his thighs guide me. His hands wandered through my hair and stroked my shoulders and I lost myself in the taste and the feel and the gorgeous energy surging between us.

Making him happy gave me joy, a rosy pink light filling me and stretching my lips in a smile even as I opened up to swallow more. His hips rocked, little waves in sync with my rhythmic moves. I pulled off him, swirling my tongue over the head, his salty pre-come a reward for my effort.

I could have kept at it a lot longer when he gripped me with both hands and pulled away. "God, stop. I'm going to lose it if you don't."

"'S okay." I reached for his hips, but he jerked aside.

"Nah, baby, this first time I want to come inside you."

He pulled me to standing, diving into my mouth with a series of ferocious kisses, shoving me against the dresser. My yoga pants evaporated and without taking his mouth off me he magic ked the condom from somewhere. I snatched the foil packet, tore it open, and stretched the rubber over him, nearly destroyed by the melting burn only his touch would relieve.

Hitching my thigh over his forearm, he ran light fingertips over my lower lips, setting off a whirlpool of shivers. I sucked on his tongue, driving my hips up, forcing his fingers inside. He took the hint and teased me, moving in and out, going deeper each time. With something close to a sob I brushed his hand aside and reached for his cock, aiming it where I needed it to be.

Groaning against my mouth, he plunged in, taking me in one strong thrust. I arched into him, jaw quivering against the burn. Yeah, it hurt, but in the best possible way, and I flashed on Krista in the bar, reminding me how good it could be.

Randy took off, rocking me, rocking the dresser, rocking the world. Every thrust radiated strength, and instead of tomboyish, I felt powerful and feminine. I might have had sex before, but this was the first time I felt like a woman doing it.

And it was *so* good.

All musicians can keep a beat, and there was definitely some motion in Randy's ocean. Pretty soon he'd doubled the pace of the waves outside, and a glorious heat started spinning from deep inside me, deeper than any man had ever reached. He gripped my neck, driving the movements of my hips with his other hand. One of us whimpered.

It was me.

He tipped his head, sweat glistening at his temples. "You're unbelievable." His words were barely more than a gasp. "You really are."

Before I could answer him, the heat grabbed me and all I could think about was faster and harder and more. On a breath, the bottom dropped out and I tumbled over a waterfall of excruciating pleasure. He slowed his pace, laughing, and asked if I was okay.

"Your turn," I said, clinging to his shoulders to keep myself upright. He reached for my other thigh, and I wrapped my legs around his waist, hitching my butt further up on the dresser.

Resting his forehead against mine, he really started to rock. His climax was so intense it all but brought me there again.

This was what I'd been missing: the sharing, the giving. We staggered over to the bunk and curled around each other, and somehow the peace in his breath against my skin made me feel like we'd been doing more than screwing a stranger. We might not quite be making love, but it was close. A deep happiness—tinged with relief—sent me drifting off to sleep.

The bunk was only wide enough for one, though, and the mattress could have doubled as a yoga mat. After a while I struggled out of the warm snuggly bed and gathered my things. Randy mumbled something at me, and I told him I was going to my own cabin. He didn't try to make me stay.

Chapter 14

Just about the time I fell asleep in my own cabin, Krista showed up. It took a solid twenty minutes for me to get more than "Tommy" and off-bombs out of her. I might even have seen a tear. Or two.

Go figure.

"What are you even doing here, anyway?" Krista had reached the pissing and grumbling stage, which I knew from experience would be followed by a flurry of texts, then sleep. She tossed herself dramatically across her bunk, phone in hand as if to verify my claim in real time.

"I just got here a little while ago." I couldn't bring myself to tell her what I'd done. I wanted to keep the beautiful memory shrouded in privacy. I mashed on my woefully understaffed pillow for a second and snuggled in. The past hurt. The future scared me.

The right now was too gorgeous for words.

I drifted off before Krista pulled far enough out of her internal vortex to ask any questions about my night.

The next morning I gave myself a break from the dress-up games and wore a pair of cotton shorts, a simple crew-neck shirt, and a pair of sturdy walking sandals, the kind with Velcro straps and a layered sole. Krista would have had a cow if she'd seen me, but she was asleep when I headed out for breakfast, so too bad for her.

I scuffed along the pathway of broken shells and gravel, headed for the lodge. Randy stood on the beach smoking a cigarette.

Breakfast could wait.

I jogged over to him, smiling like a middle-school girl. I had my hands on him before he even turned around, and went up on tiptoe to give him a big ol' morning smooch.

He tipped his head at the last second and I bussed his cheek.

"Morning," I said, though his reserved expression damped my smile.

"Hi."

His tone was flat, off. "What's up?" I asked.

"Nothing." Moving slowly, like something hurt, he shifted toward the ocean. "Just…nothing."

One of my hands fluttered like a bird who didn't quite know where to land. "I was …" I squelched a sudden sob. "Just headed in to breakfast."

"Sure. Sounds good." He took my hand, just like he would have before. He walked with me to the lodge, just like he would have before. He even nuzzled my ear and murmured something not quite intelligible. When others could see. His behavior was the same, but his energy was utterly, completely different.

The dining room was crowded and we grabbed a couple of seats at one of the big tables on the perimeter. Right after we sat, Pregnant Sue and Jessica Freeman claimed the last two open chairs. They shared smiles with several of our table-mates, a cross-section of teachers from different ages and genders and fashion orientations. People made innocuous conversation, and Randy sat silent, and I let my eggs get cold.

"Are there many sessions you want to see today?" he finally asked.

"A few."

He swallowed some coffee and gave me a crooked smile. "I've got to go to my cabin for a minute. Let's connect at lunch, okay?"

"'Kay." Probably take me that long to get all the hurt cried out of my system. He pressed a kiss on the top of my head on this way to standing and before I could respond, he strode out of the room.

I kept a placid smile in place, though it cut my heart out to do it. See, getting stood up at the altar had taught me a thing or two about handling rejection. I had no idea what had twisted Randy all sideways, but I'd be damned if I let him make me look bad in front of my colleagues.

I was still shoving eggs around when Jessica started talking.

"So did you and Randy start"—she tapped her fork on one side of her plate, and then the other, making a meaningless gesture feel dirty—"seeing each other, I mean, before this weekend?"

I straightened my shoulders and stared her down the way I would an annoying helicopter parent. "Before."

"Oh good." She covered her heart with her hand. "Because you know how guys like him are."

I lowered my fork with as much care as I could muster, a safer choice than stabbing her in the eyes.

"I mean, I'm sure he's changed." Her smile had so much slime in it I half started looking for tadpoles.

"He's a nice guy," I said, willing this conversation to end before the tears flooding my heart leaked out all over the table.

"Oh, very nice. Very, very nice." Two-handed pat-down for emphasis. "It's just, well, he might have hooked up with someone at this event before." Her prom queen glow said she enjoyed eviscerating me. "But I'm pretty sure he didn't even ask for her phone number afterwards."

Placid smile. Placid smile. Placid smile. Placid, placid, placid. Don't freak out.

She and Pregnant Sue cleared their dishes away and sailed across the room. I exhaled and caught the eye of the woman sitting next to me. "The food's been pretty good this weekend, don't you think?"

She agreed, and I stuffed a forkful of pretty good eggs in my mouth and managed not to spew across the table. One voice in my head was calling her a liar, since Randy'd never been to this retreat before.

Another voice kept pointing out that so far he hadn't asked for my phone number, either.

Chapter 15

"We're still going to see the band tonight, right?" Krista asked. She and I were in the lobby near the big stone fireplace. Randy stood behind me with his hands on my shoulders, leaning against the paneled wall.

"I think we should," he said. He lifted my hair and blew on the secret spot behind my ear. He was acting normal—or what passed for normal in the forty-eight hours since we'd met.

One of the other teachers heard us talking about the band, and pretty soon everyone around thought they might join us. Including Jessica Freeman's new chinless appendage, Kirk.

I almost vetoed the whole project, but Krista argued J-Bone would protect us and Randy pointed out most everyone was going straight home after the conference ended, so their talk about seeing the band was just talk.

My sense of humor would have been sturdier if Randy hadn't taken his little trip through crazy. Even though he'd spent the afternoon at my side, a solid, affectionate presence, I couldn't shake the sense of distance he'd created on the beach. Ever since Creighton left me standing alone in my one-of-a-kind Alençon lace dress, I'd been more inclined to be the one to dash first.

Everyone attended the last session, and afterward people were still buzzing about the band in Langley. *Fantastic.* Krista had more to pack than I did, so after loading my gear into the CRV I went for a walk on the beach. Barefoot, because at Krista's insistence, I'd put on the little stretchy black thing she'd picked out for me at Target. The dress left very little to the imagination, and of course I had to borrow her chunky black heels.

When I got back, still carrying the heels, Randy waited on the front porch of my cabin. I slowed my pace, feeling like a marionette, all twitchy motions and jangling limbs. My fight-or-flight reflex engaged. He hadn't asked for my phone number, he'd pushed me away, this was all just a damned act.

Run!

The late-day sun warmed my shoulders, and he squinted as I got closer. "I told Krista I'd give you a ride," he said, "so she took off in your car."

"Yeah, she had my keys." My voice sounded tight, as if pieces of it might flake away like the silvery scales of a fish. "I'll just turn in the cabin key and we can go."

Randy followed me to the lodge. I tossed my key into a basket on the check-in table and bumped into him when I turned around. He smelled good, soap and woodsy cologne layered over the persistent scent of cigarette smoke. I couldn't meet his eyes.

He brushed a stray hair off my forehead. For once I didn't have my hair in a ponytail or a knot. It hung long to my shoulders, with a thin black band holding my bangs out of my face. "You look amazing. Everything okay?"

"Sure." I smiled at his right ear and slid into the heels.

He nodded and, taking my hand, led me out of the cabin towards the parking lot. I couldn't help notice how well his black T-shirt fit. Almost as nice as his faded jeans, and I about swallowed my tongue when he went to the driver's door of a cherry red Chevy Malibu.

"What year is this thing?" Climbing into the passenger seat of such a cool car was almost spiritual.

"1970." He gunned the engine like it was a rocket and we were ready to launch.

It was going to be a long night.

Langley was about halfway between the lodge and the ferry dock. One of the bigger small towns on Whidbey Island, it had a reputation for welcoming tourists. The locals were an eclectic mix, ranging from yuppies who commuted to jobs in Seattle to subsistence-farming hippies who supplied the weekend market and craft fair. I'd never been there before, and never expected my first trip there would be in a cherry red Malibu with a Ginger God at the wheel.

We drove through the forest with the windows open, both because of the heat and so Randy could smoke. His damp hair still showed comb marks and he'd trimmed his beard a little, enough to take the roughest edges off. I stared out the window, shooting occasional glances at him like BBs from a gun, quick darts to keep from giving anything away.

He took one last drag off his cigarette and dropped the butt into an empty soda can. It sizzled, suggesting the can wasn't entirely empty. "Only two more."

"Two?"

"I'm allowed five a day."

Self-righteousness gave me the confidence to examine his profile. "So you'll get lung cancer more slowly."

"Something like that." His grin flipped something south of my navel. "I don't drink because I can't, and I smoke because I can."

And I don't want this to end, because you're one of the coolest men I've ever met. We cleared the woods and headed through the rural equivalent of a subdivision, low ranch houses scattered along the road, reachable by long straight driveways.

I leaned into the channel-back vinyl seat, trying to figure out a way to tell him I'd be okay if he wanted to drop the act so we could just hang out like friends. Or, to be accurate, new acquaintances. I'd gotten laid, after all, and Kirk had moved on to a more interested woman.

Mission accomplished.

Instead I kept my mouth shut, tossing BB glances at him and feeling like an idiot.

He stroked the back of my hand with his thumb, which totally distracted me. The sun was low enough that the cars coming toward us along the two-lane road had their headlights on. Letting go of my hand, he flipped up the visor and caught me in his side-eye. "I had fun last night."

His comment got my attention like a sharp yank on my collar. "Me too." My voice was pitifully weak, and for just a second, I hoped the whole bar would be full of music teachers so maybe I could avoid him.

As if avoiding him would fix anything.

He started to say something. Stopped. Started. Stopped. Finally brought my hand to his lips for a kiss, accompanied by a self-conscious laugh.

We rode in silence until reaching one of the rare traffic lights, where we stopped to make the turn to Langley. It would have been the perfect time to ask what had happened this morning, or if he intended to call me after tomorrow, or if I should just hold onto my memories and wait for my Academy Award.

My phone chirped, saving me from doing anything difficult. Krista texted me directions to the pub. I almost managed to relay the information without sounding like a total dork.

Chapter 16

A crowd of locals filled most of the club's seats, but Krista had snagged us a table. The Blues Revivalists had already started playing their brand of rowdy blues rock. J-Bone was MIA, which didn't surprise me. Didn't seem to surprise Krista, either, or even bother her too much. She divided her attention between pouring beer from our pitcher and grinning at a guy with dreadlocks at a table to our right.

The pub's walls were covered with posters advertising upcoming shows, and a flat-screen TV over the bar showed a preseason Seahawks game. I couldn't relax, despite the party atmosphere. Randy talked to Krista, which covered the uptight silence rolling off me. When the band took a break, one of the guitar players came over. Randy greeted him with an awkward back-thumping guy hug. After a round of introductions, Mike grabbed a chair and pulled it close, leaning across me so he could talk to Randy.

"You got your horn, man? Wanna sit in?" Mike asked, checking me out like he wanted to find a place to bite. Randy draped an arm across my shoulders, pulling me close and marking his territory, and since my dress would have worked in an anatomy class, I didn't mind at all.

"No horn," Randy said, his rough voice right by my ear. The skin on my neck prickled, excitement amplified by nerves.

Mike crossed his arms, showing off the classic anchor he had tattooed on one forearm, like Popeye but dirtier. "Keys, then. We can boot Sanders off for a couple of tunes."

"Okay if I play a couple?" Randy asked me.

"Sure."

Giving my shoulders a squeeze, he followed Mike to the stage. I watched him go, admiring the view from behind, then turned to get a face full of pissed-off Krista.

"What's wrong with you?" Her hissing whisper cut through the hubbub of the crowd around us. "Until Mike showed up, you were sitting there like you had a rod up your ass. Did Randy do something to piss you off?"

"No. I don't know." I did my best to pull it together. "What if he's acting?"

"Oh shit. He's *so* not." Krista's laugh dumped a bucket of reality over my internal drama-fest. "If you could have seen the look on his face when Mike sat down and started checking you out…he's not acting," she said. "Definitely not."

"Then why hasn't he asked for my phone number?" I hugged myself and glanced at the stage. From behind the keyboard, Randy made snarky comments to the drummer. He acted more comfortable on stage than any place else I'd seen him. Mike the biker made a lame joke, the bass player ran a scale, and the drummer counted off a tune. I couldn't see Randy's hands on the keys, but the set of his shoulders and the passion in his eyes reminded me of Creighton, the one who'd left me hamstrung by memories.

Those memories were nothing compared with the emotional whirlwind created by the guy on stage.

The band's opening chords were timed with J-Bone's arrival. Krista reeled him in and gave him a peck on the cheek, her semi-satisfied smirk a subtle indicator of her happiness. He'd brought a friend, too, Micky or Nicky or something. They were pretty much a matched set of 24-Hour Fitness beefcake, and I smiled politely and tried to ignore the fact they both seemed to think we were on a double date.

In the middle of the next song, Krista threw a balled-up napkin at me and gestured at the stage. "He's really, really good," she said. "Right?"

Randy took the band to another level, his rolling left hand giving them extra swing. His first solo threw down a challenge the rest of them tried to meet, and his chops had me lubricated in ways I'd never imagined. The band blazed through three songs before Randy shook hands all around.

And he walked off stage and out of the bar without sparing me a glance.

Surprise and confusion held me in my seat.

"Where's he going?" Krista unwrapped herself from J-Bone long enough to give me a *WTF* shrug.

I mirrored her, eyebrows raised, palms up. "Don't know."

"Follow him."

I propped my elbows on the table and dropped my head into my hands. Seriously? Why the drama? Micky-Nicky put his beefy hand on the bare skin between my shoulder blades. "Wassup?"

Krista bounced something off the top of my head. "Follow him."

"Yeah." I still didn't move, except to shrug off the creeping hand. Maybe he just went to smoke a cigarette and he'd be right back. Five minutes passed. Ten. No Randy.

Krista reached across the table and used two fingers to lift my forehead so she could look me in the eye. "Listen, I'm clearly not an expert on relationships, but if you blow this you're going to regret it for a long, long time."

Regret what? Regret a man whom I'd never heard of until forty-eight hours ago? Regret a man who couldn't seem to make up his mind whether he liked me or not?

Regret a man who took a casual hookup and made me feel like we were making love?

There was something real between us, and the surprise and shock and confusion gave way to a white-hot anger. I shook off the beefcake and surged out of my chair. How *dare* he take off without saying anything?

Outside the bar, antique and faux-antique storefronts all sat one wide sidewalk off the street, with a solid line of cars parked in both directions. Randy stood about half a block away, under a street light with a couple of other smokers. For the first time all night, I was glad to be wearing a pair of high heels.

They made stalking much easier.

Randy saw me coming, though his expression didn't change. I kept my pace slow, swinging my arms to shake off some energy. My gut was coiled so tight I had to lock my jaw to keep in a scream. He took a long drag off his cigarette and dropped the butt, crushing it with his heel.

"Where's your date?" he asked.

I took a white-knuckle grip on the hem of my skirt to keep from belting him one. "Um…you are. Or did I misunderstand something?"

He shoved a hand in his pocket like he was going to go for another cigarette. "Listen, Maggie, you're beautiful and smart and funny, and this is just not going to work."

His words rolled over me like little razor blades. I should have known someone as cool as Randy wouldn't be interested in me.

Except, wait a minute. *He likes me. I know he does.* My courage was struggling like a salmon going upstream, but I decided to give it one more try.

"What's not going to work?" I got close to him, close enough to smell the woodsy, spicy man under the halo of smoke. "It's not going to work for us to hear a band play on a Sunday night?"

He pressed his lips together, most of his face hidden in the shadows cast by the streetlights. In my heels I wasn't quite eye-level with him, but close. I locked his gaze with mine, daring him to ignore me. "Or it's not going to work for us to spend the night in a hotel room? Because you know I have the key."

"Shit." He rubbed a thumb over my lower lip, then tipped his head like he was moving against his will.

Or against his own better judgment.

I didn't move until he kissed me, and then I grabbed a hold with both hands. I'd never kissed angry before, but I did this time, and it was cold, and raw, and bruising. His scruff of a beard burned my chin and his hands were on me tighter than the stupid black dress and his erection jammed into my thigh. Hungry for more, I bit his lower lip hard enough to make him groan.

He pulled away, fists against either side of my face. "Hotel?"

"Yeah."

Chapter 17

Krista had given me the card for the room with the promise she'd crash someplace with J-Bone. The hotel was about four blocks from the bar, and we covered the distance silently, barely touching. *Fine*. If Randy only wanted sex, that was all he'd get.

I swiped us into the room, where the generic, faux-country decor could have come from any hotel in any city. Silently I snatched at his shirt, lifting it high enough to rub my palms over his bare skin.

In retaliation, he ripped the zipper down and dragged off my little black dress. His action left me breathing hard and naked except for a thong and those god-awful heels. I got my hands in his hair and hammered him with furious kisses, humping his cock through his jeans. I dragged on his shirt until the fabric started to rip and he yanked it over his head. For a second he had both arms in the air and tangled in fabric and I grasped his hardness with both hands. So wanting. So eager.

Randy jerked away, throwing his shirt across the room and grabbing hold of my wrists. He seized my hands and pinned them behind me, sucking and biting the tender skin on my neck in a ferocious barrage until with a garbled cry I begged him to stop. Or keep going.

Keep going.

He backed me up till my knees hit the bed. Determined to bring him down first, I twisted, trying to get some leverage, but he forced me onto my butt. I propped myself on my elbows and spread my legs, unsure who was the predator and who was the prey. It might be another five years and however many months before I had another man between my knees, and I meant to make it good this time.

He took his glasses off and tossed them in the general direction of his shirt. Without the shield, the heat of his gaze scorched wherever it touched. I wanted to lick the turbulent colors of his gorgeous dragon tattoo, to taste the snake as it crossed his lower belly. My pulse throbbed in my overheated lady parts. He popped the top button on his jeans and I sighed, or whimpered, or something equally embarrassing.

To get back at him, I slid a hand low over my belly, nudging aside the sheer lace of my thong. The tension in his jaw said he was properly provoked. "There's a raincoat in my purse," I said.

He snorted a laugh. "Yes, mistress."

A minute later he threw a packet onto my belly. I let it lie there, counting down from 100 to keep from moving first.

I made it to eighty-seven before a muffled "fuck" told me Randy had reached his limit. He shucked his jeans and he grasped my thong by the crotch, yanking until one of the side bands gave way. It left a mark like a tiny whiplash across my thigh. He got the condom on one-handed and thrust inside me faster than I could process what had happened. Then he shoved my calves over his shoulders and rose up on his knees.

Eyes shut and head rocked back, Randy slammed into me, very much the Ginger God. He groaned with every thrust, going deeper than I'd ever experienced. He moved his hips in a slow circle, spinning me tighter than tight. My fists' bitter grip on the bedspread kept me together until it didn't, and I shattered in a scream of pleasure.

He dropped forward to his elbows but didn't stop thrusting. His body made a cage, trapping me, pinning me, equal parts safety and danger. He rocked harder, faster, head burrowed under my jaw, groans turning to heavy grunts.

"Now." He gasped and stilled, buried so deep he had to be leaving some of himself behind.

We lay there for several long moments, until he lifted my hand and laid it on the center of his chest, covering it with his own. "You damage me, baby. Right here."

I shoved him off and ran into the bathroom, afraid to let him to see me cry.

I didn't cry, but I didn't come out, either.

"Maggie?" One word, accompanied by a soft tap on the door. "Baby, are you okay?"

Randy's voice was husky and raw, a perfect match for my soul. Still I waited, my eyes closed, my hand on the doorknob. *Deep breath*. I turned the handle. Released. The door yielded, swinging slowly open as if propelled by our intensity alone.

I stepped into the room. He encircled me, held me, murmured soft and indistinct words in my ear. After a long time, longer than I'd waited for him in the bar, longer than I'd hidden in the bathroom, his thumb stroked my cheek. I lifted my head. Our lips met, so soft. Tender. As if we both knew we'd never kiss like this again.

He drew me to the bed and again we made love, this time slow, deliberate. Taking as much time as we needed, as much time as we had. His tongue wrapped around mine. My fingers threaded through his ginger curls. Our breath mingled. He paused before he entered me, his fingers tracing patterns on my belly, my legs spread wide. He slid home and I curled around him, wanting it never to end.

But with every gasp, every taste, every thrust, I knew we were saying goodbye.

Afterward, when he fell asleep, I tugged my black dress over my head, slipped my feet into Krista's killer heels, and left.

Because anything we tried to say would just make it hurt even worse.

Chapter 18

"What do you mean you just left?"

I excused Krista's shout of laughter because it was three thirty in the morning and we were both a little hysterical. "I couldn't stay. He felt so good, and it hurt so bad."

"You stole that line from a Hallmark card." She groaned and flipped the lever to recline her seat. We were in my CRV, parked outside the hotel where I'd left Randy.

In the room Krista and I were paying for.

"I can't believe we're both out here." I'd locked myself in the CRV shorty after coming out of the bathroom and finding Randy asleep, and Krista had scared the piss out of me when she'd knocked on the window.

"We're lame." She shut her eyes as if she expected to snooze.

I'd accidentally dozed off once or twice , but a woman alone in a car at night would be stupid to relax, even in a hotel parking lot. With two of us out here, I felt safer. I reclined my seat and closed my eyes.

"J-Bone is such an asshole," Krista murmured, half asleep already.

"Mmm."

"I mean, at least Randy admitted he had feelings for you."

I roused enough to glare at her. "He said I damaged him."

"In his heart."

"Shut up." Too far gone to interpret oblique references, I only knew I couldn't be near him if he intended to leave me behind. He was strong, beautiful, talented, funny—everything I wanted.

And he'd never even asked for my damned phone number.

Not that I was obsessed or anything.

"You know," I said, raising a grunt out of Krista, "I'm an idiot, because I thought getting laid would make me feel better about myself, and I feel like shit."

She turned her head toward me and opened one eye. "You were only supposed to fuck him, not fall in love."

Oh yeah. That.

Without answering her, I shut my eyes and tried to relax. And really did sleep, for a while, until the morning sun stabbed my face and dragged me into tomorrow.

I wanted to catch the first ferry home, but though all my stuff was in the CRV, Krista's was still in our hotel room. We found a Denny's restaurant and shared a Grand Slam Breakfast and a couple of bloody Marys. Properly fortified in case of a man sighting, we returned to the hotel.

The room was empty.

"Of course he left, the sneaky, evil—"

"Um, you left him first." Krista smacked the back of my head on the way by. "You should take your slut clothes off before we get on the ferry."

She lent me a vintage housedress with cabbage roses and buttons in the front, and I handed over her black heels. I walked barefoot to the car and helped her load her stuff. I felt sick, and vacant, like instead of scratching an itch, the time I'd spent with Randy had dug a crater.

Once everything was in, I took a deep breath and put the car in gear. My exhale came out sounding awful close to a sigh.

"It doesn't have to end, you know," Krista said.

"Oh right, like he's going to make a psychic connection to my cell phone."

"He's a public school teacher, for pity's sake. You know which school he's at. Look him up on their website. Call the district office. Hell, ask around till you find someone who knows him."

I bit my lower lip to keep from telling her off. She was right, but I was in too shitty a mood to admit it. We drove in silence along the winding road from Langley to the town of Clinton, where the ferry docked. Fortunately, the crowd was thin and it didn't take long to pay our fare and get in line.

About four cars behind a cherry red 1970 Chevy Malibu.

Using every ounce of willpower, I shut the engine off instead of throwing the transmission into reverse. Krista wouldn't necessarily recognize Randy's car, so I kept my mouth shut. She had her cell phone out for a brief flurry of texts. *Good. Keep her occupied.* Randy climbed out of the car and walked across the holding lot to the espresso stand.

I shrunk down, hoping he wouldn't see me, which drew her attention. "What?"

"Nothing."

She sat straighter and spotted him in about eight and a half seconds. "No shit."

"Just…don't …"

"Oh, I'm not." She pocketed her cell phone and shifted in her seat to face me. Everything about her was hard, the edge of her bangs, her bold glasses, the thin line of her lips. "You know what you need to do."

"What?" Apologize for leaving? Give him my phone number just so I could feel better about it? Beg him to give us a chance? *Wow*. No easy choices there.

Something bumped the hood of my car. Kirk and Jessica, walking arm in arm from wherever they'd parked, headed for the espresso stand. Krista made a disgusted sound, and it dawned on me the only reason he'd messed around with me was to piss Jessica off. *Great.* Now I could add humiliation to my emotional shit-storm.

A sunbeam bounced off the Malibu's chrome trim. Resting my head on the steering wheel, I closed my eyes and interlaced my fingers, clutching hard enough to cut little half-moons with my nails. I wasn't some scared girl using a softball bat to keep her heart safe. Was I?

Randy was either scared shitless or a complete dirtbag. We might have started playing a game, but my gut said the heat between us was real, so I decided to put my money on "terrified." If I was wrong, I could always pick up my ball and glove and go home.

My move.

"There's a Sharpie marker in the glove box. Could you reach it for me?"

Krista's eyebrow rose like she thought I'd clearly gone cuckoo. "Sharpie in your glove box?"

"Grade school teacher."

Both eyebrows went up, but she didn't say anything. She handed me the marker and I tossed her the keys. "I'll either be right back, or I'll see you on the other side."

I stuffed the marker in the pocket of the dress, got out of the CRV, and walked over to the Malibu, my heart hammering louder than every bagpipe ever played. Randy met me at the driver's side door.

"Can I have your keys, please?" I asked.

The high overcast reflected silver off his glasses, but his expression was wary. "Okay."

I got in the driver's side, and he got in the passenger's side, and we sat there in absolute silence for what felt like an hour. I had no agenda, just a heart full of desire I didn't want to waste.

"I'm sorry I—"

"I'm sorry, Maggie—"

We spoke over each other and stopped at the same time.

"I shouldn't have left—" I started again.

"The bar." He finished for me.

This time we laughed. He took hold of my hand and dragged my fingertips through his stubble before planting a kiss on my palm.

"We're both forgiven, then."

"Yeah." His lips moved against my skin, sending a thrill through my core. "For a guy who doesn't do drugs, I can sure act like a fool."

My answer was lost in the blast of the ferry's horn and the rumble of automobile engines all around us.

"Well, if you're going to drive this thing, it's time to go," he said.

I turned the key in the ignition and put it in drive.

Chapter 19

The Malibu drove like a boat. The shocks were soft and the brakes were crisp and the front end was at least three times as long as the CRV. We followed the line of cars onto the ferry, but after we parked, I stopped Randy from getting out. In my CRV, I could have locked his door from my control pad. As it was, I used my teacher's voice.

"Can't leave until this is settled."

It worked. He stayed put. I waited until all the other passengers cleared the car deck, my palms sweating and my mouth as dry as if I'd been sucking on sponge. Randy sat with his arms crossed, jaw tight, expression shielded.

When the car deck emptied and the ferry got underway, I scooted across the bench seat toward Randy.

"Listen, this has been a really great weekend," he said.

I cut him off with a palm over his mouth. "Yep." I got my left hip free of the steering wheel and swung my leg up, straddling him. I was so far past my normal comfort zone I might have been breathing helium instead of the steel and rubber old car smell.

"Now, here's the deal." I pulled his shirt up, baring his belly.

"Hey, now."

His protest faded in laughter, and I took the marker in hand. "It would have been much easier," I said as I started scrawling numbers across his flat abdomen, "if you'd just asked for my effing telephone number."

I finished with my initials and a smiley face.

He looked at my handiwork, then at me. "Point taken." He pulled me closer, working his hands under my skirt. "I don't usually ask for a woman's phone number, because I don't usually intend to call."

"Oh, oops." I brought fingertips to my lips like Betty Boop gone crazy. "Guess you'll have to make an exception in my case."

"I guess"—he ran a fingertip along my collar, stopping at the button right above my cleavage—"since you've forced the issue"—he flicked the button, the hardness in his groin swelling—"I'll have to."

I leaned forward and nipped his bottom lip. He dragged me even closer, crushing my mouth to his. He kissed me, hard and hot, until I was ready for more. I scooted my butt toward his knees, my hand on his fly, giving myself room to work.

"Are you sure you want to do this?"

"I have a rubber."

"No, baby, I mean this, like, get involved with a guy with my kind of baggage?"

I made a big show of thinking through his question before working down the zipper in his fly. "The ferry's going to dock in ten, maybe fifteen minutes, I don't have any panties on, and you are the hottest guy I've ever met, ever, in my life." His cock sprang free and I got a firm grip on its solid length. "Ever."

I made quick work of sliding the condom into place, and even quicker work of sliding *him* into place. Our heads fell together naturally, resting on each other's shoulders. I rode him slow and easy, though it didn't take long till he pinned my hips in place and quickened the pace. Waves of heated pleasure built, and crested, and surged again. He brought his thumb over the spot where my body joined his and started to rub, and I almost wept it felt so good.

There was something healing in the private bubble we created in his old car. The motion of the ferry moving over the water, and of our bodies moving together, solidified our connection. With him so deep inside, I couldn't be dishonest, couldn't be anyone but myself.

And I loved him. Maybe I couldn't say the words, but the feeling was real.

The rhythm between us shifted again, speeding, tightening, till I crashed over him in a climax so strong I couldn't make a sound. He followed me with a heavy humming growl, thrusting so hard I bonked my head on the roof of the car.

When we could catch our breath, we laughed, soft and intimate. "I thought I would die," he said, "when I woke up and you were gone."

"I'm so sorry." I cupped his cheek. "I thought you only wanted sex." Rubbing his lips with my thumb, I tried to pull my thoughts together. "We were acting, but we weren't really, but then we were again." I squinched my face. "That didn't come out right."

He chuckled, the kind of low, happy sound I could listen to forever. "I know what you mean. I don't think either of us expected"—he kissed me as gently as the late summer sun on the water—"this."

"This," I echoed.

"I knew what I wanted from the first time I kissed you, but I never thought you'd want me," he said. "Which is why, you know, I acted like an asshole half the time."

"Perhaps not the most effective strategy for attracting a woman." I rocked my hips and he hissed, already half-hard.

"Next time you try to pull a disappearing act," I said, "I'm going grab you by the balls and hang on."

He wrapped both hands around my butt and pulled me closer. "You do that."

We both startled when the first passengers came past the window, and did our best to straighten ourselves without giving anyone a free show. We had to crawl all over each other to switch seats so Randy could drive, and he ended up taking me all the way home.

Because there was no place else either of us wanted to be.

About the Author

Liv Rancourt writes light, funny, contemporary romance and urban fantasy. Her novel *Hell…The Story* was a 2014 Amazon Breakthrough Novel Award quarterfinal entry. Previous publishing credits include *Forever & Ever, Amen; A Vampire's Deadly Delight;* and several short stories in the *Ten Tales* series.

Liv's day job is as a neonatal nurse practitioner, and she's taken care of small and sick infants for almost thirty years. Before she got serious about writing, she spent her free time fronting a rock band and hanging out in the church choir. Currently, she lives in Seattle with her husband, two teenagers, two ferrets, one crabby cat, and one sweet puppy.

She can be found online at her website and blog (*www.livrancourt.com*), on Facebook (*www.facebook.com/liv.rancourt*), or on Twitter (*www.twitter.com/LivRancourt*).

More from This Author
(From *Forever and Ever, Amen* by Liv Rancourt)

Between her ex and her job and her teenagers, there weren't many chances for fun in Molly's life. The one guaranteed bright spot was Friday Happy Hour with her best friend Sam, when they met at Coopers, the kind of place where it was too dark to see the dirt. The bartenders played '80s music, which helped them pretend they were back in college as they rocked out to the B52s or Pat Benatar.

Over the years they'd come to an understanding. Molly knew what it cost Sam to balance her kids, her husband and her work, and Sam knew all about Ford. Or as much as Molly was willing to tell her.

But this week they made an exception. They planned to meet at The Mystic, the new "it" restaurant in town. It was a spare and modern place that still managed to be comfortable, though their fellow diners were mostly young and beautiful, which made Molly feel old and—well, old. The floor was polished concrete and the furnishings had an industrial look that was softened with velvet cushions. The first cocktail Molly ordered had lavender liqueur in it, and the little pupu plates on the menu combined small bites with lush sauces and truffle oil that looked more like art than food.

"So did Diana torture you today?" Sam usually started off with a question about work so Molly could get it off her chest. Molly was the human resources manager for a medium-sized medical supply company, and Sam job-shared a project manager position for a graphics firm. Part-time work was a concession to having four kids, although her lawyer husband earned enough that she didn't really need to work at all.

"No, thank God. She took the afternoon off so I actually got some stuff done." The waiter brought their appetizer—tiny tarts filled with a deep orange substance that the menu called tomato foam and topped with a swirl of brilliant green pesto.

"What was she on about this week?" Sam asked.

"The usual. She's all hot to get the Dallas scores up, to show that we have happy employees." Molly shrugged. "I figure if we pay them, they ought to be happy."

Sam smiled, giving Molly another opportunity to envy her lovely coral lips and the faint brush of peach on her cheekbones. Sam always wore makeup. They'd been sisters at Chi Omega and stayed friends after college. Sam's straight, fawn-colored hair was usually pulled back in a ponytail, although once or twice Molly had seen it down. She'd never seen her without the lipstick, which Sam treated like a religious ritual. "Diana must get a bonus if you raise the scores."

"Good for her. She rides me like a pony and then she gets the money." Molly tipped her head up to catch the waiter's eye. "I think I need one more."

Sam picked up the drink menu. It was printed on heavy cardstock with a hand scrawled list of fancy cocktails. "Maybe the bartender makes it up as he goes along," she said, thinking out loud as she scanned it. "Let's try the one called Satan's Whiskers."

Molly, too, scanned the menu. "I'm not sure what gin and Satan have in common, but okay."

While they waited for their drinks, Sam brought up one of her favorite topics. "So, you hate your job, right?"

"Come on, Sam, I know where this is going."

"And your husband is in the 35 percent tax bracket, right?"

"Knock it off." Molly stared out the window, shutting her friend out. This conversation was more of a rhetorical exercise, an area they'd basically agreed to disagree on. That didn't stop Sam from bringing it up every week.

The glare from the headlights on First Avenue turned the big windows into mirrors. Molly could see a slice of herself perched like a bird between the young and trendy diners that surrounded them. Her short curly hair had dried right for a change, and she wore a tailored black suit softened by the green silk of her blouse, a color chosen to play up her bright blue eyes. If it had really been a mirror, she would have picked over the crow's-feet and scattered gray in her curls. Instead, she waited for Sam to get to the end of her lecture.

"Quit dodging. File already."

"I'm not dodging." Molly met Sam's gaze head-on. "Ford owns the courtroom."

"He wouldn't dare mess with you. It'd be too easy to dig up dirt on him. And fuck it, sometimes you need to stand up to the things that scare you."

Hearing the F-bomb drop from Sam's perfect lips always made Molly smile. "Sky down, girlfriend. It's not worth it."

"Right. Whatever."

Sam sounded distracted, which was surprising. Usually she was good for several more rounds of the "you really need to file" game. Sam was the only one who knew that Molly and Ford's "divorce" was more of an informal separation, a gentleman's agreement, and Molly planned to keep it that way.

She noticed her friend staring at something across the room and figured talking about her kids would bring her back. "Is Patrice working on an application for St. Boniface?"

"Later. Don't turn around." Sam spoke through her teeth and smiled at the waiter as he passed them their drinks. Molly's head twitched in the direction Sam was staring, because that's what happened whenever someone told her not to turn around. "Don't," Sam hissed.

"What is it that I'm not supposed to be looking at?" Molly asked as she took a sip of Satan's Whiskers. The citrusy gin cocktail wasn't all that strong, or else the first one was already getting to her.

"There's a guy at the bar and he's been checking you out since we got here."

"Doubtful. I'm not that interesting." Molly leaned back and laughed. "We're the wrong generation for that kind of action here."

"He's worked himself up to smiling. I'm going to go bring him over." Sam half stood in her chair.

"Ah, hello, mother of four and happily married."

"Not for me, for you. You ain't got nothing a good lay won't cure." Grinning at her own joke, Sam headed toward the bar.

"Spoken like a woman who's given birth four times," Molly said to herself. She slowly turned around to see where her friend was going. Sam's camel-colored wool slacks retained a knife pleat down the back, as if they'd just come from the dry cleaners, and her creamy silk blouse was barely wrinkled.

Molly had envied Sam's polish since she was nineteen years old. With Sam's curves, all it took to change her tailored daytime vibe to something more sophisticated was to unbutton the top couple buttons on her blouse. Molly watched Sam approach the man at the bar. When she turned around those two buttons were undone.

Sam played it up by laughing, chin up and shoulders back so he could get a glimpse down her cleavage. After a couple minutes, she led the guy toward their table. He looked smooth, as if he crossed the bar to meet strange women all the time. His caramel skin, black hair and dark lashes suggested he was from the Middle East somewhere—maybe India—and he wore a deep red turtleneck with jeans and a leather jacket.

"Molly, this is…oh, I'm so embarrassed. What did you say your name was?" A blush bloomed under Sam's Perfect Peach makeup.

"So pleased to meet you, Molly." He took her hands and planted an air kiss near it. At Sam's invitation, he joined them at their table.

Tall and dark had always been Molly's type, and as the stranger settled into the chair next to her, Molly felt her eyes open just a bit wider and her breath get short. It was uncomfortably close to the way Ford made her feel.

"You ladies are unaccompanied," the stranger said. His voice sounded like it had been rubbed by steel wool.

"That's a three dollar word for Girls Night Out," Sam laughed.

Molly sat there with a ruler running up her spine and a foolish grin. She watched Sam elegantly swirl the remains of her Satan's Whiskers cocktail. Sam had always been the boy-magnet.

"May I buy you another?" The stranger gestured at Sam's glass.

"Actually, my, uh, nanny just texted me." Sam tossed off the rest of her drink. "I've got to go home and deal with a science project that's gone awry."

"Is everybody okay?" Molly was like an aunt to Sam's kids, and their constant escapades left her with a mix of humor and worry, though in this instance she suspected there was no real problem at home.

Sam pushed away from the table. "Only a little blood. Sorry to bag on you, Mol. I'll call you tomorrow."

And that quickly she was gone, leaving the slightly tipsy Molly with a strange guy in an unfamiliar setting. Molly was still deciding how to proceed when the stranger leaned in closer. His scent, a rich mix of aftershave and MAN, in capital letters, sparked something down below her belly button.

Molly shifted in her chair, looking for some breathing room. He was a little intimidating, and not just because he was so much taller than her. "What did you say your name was, again?"

"Where's your husband?"

This time she edged the chair away. "I asked you first."

He laughed, a mellow sound compared with the gruffness of his voice. Molly's spine softened.

"Okay, well, since you're being secretive, I won't tell you where my husband is, either." Molly reached for her drink, hoping her hand was steady enough not to spill.

"You don't want to know."

"You're probably right." Molly laughed and managed to take a sip of her drink. Like this guy actually knew where her husband was. It didn't bear thinking about. "What are you doing here, anyway? Guys our age don't usually make lateral moves."

"Lateral?"

"You know, hitting on someone who's old enough to have been your prom date. Usually a guy like you wants some twenty-something pretty to help him deal with the midlife blues."

The words were out of her mouth before she knew it. If nothing else, Satan's Whiskers had put her internal editor to sleep. She watched nervously for his response.

Fortunately, he just raised an eyebrow and smiled instead of getting huffy. "You know little about men."

"I know as much as I need to." If her sleeping editor let some extra bitterness into her words, Molly ignored it. She placed her forearms on the table and leaned toward her new friend, torn between the desire to trace his lips with the tip of her finger and the fear that he might bite. She credited the fear to his resemblance to Ford.

He laughed and flagged down the waiter. "We'll see."

Molly trailed a finger down the hand-written cocktail menu instead, debating whether she had the intestinal fortitude for another round of Satan's Whiskers. She glanced up to see the stranger staring at her, his gaze uncomfortably intense in the restaurant's candle demi-light. "Red?" she asked.

"Pardon."

"Your eyes are red."

He blinked slowly and his smile faded. Before he could speak, the waiter came to their table. The stranger ordered them another round of cocktails, and after that the night slid into a crazy patchwork dream, the kind where things were disagreeable but too muddled for Molly to feel real fear. There was some drinking that might have involved tequila, some nervous laughter, and more of that warm feeling down below. She did remember that, more than once, when the light hit the stranger's eyes at just the right angle, they turned scarlet, like staring into the heart of a fire. They left the bar, things got blurrier, then Molly woke up in her own bed, and for some reason it was noisy.

• • •

"Mom? Mom, wake up." Molly heard pounding on the door. Her daughter's voice sounded like it came from Pluto. "Mom?"

The bedroom door cracked open just as Molly pulled her eyelids apart. She had to shut her left eye to focus her right, but when she did she saw a slice of Flora's worried face peeking into her room. "I'm here," Molly whispered, because that's all the sound she could make.

"It's like eleven thirty." Flora pushed the door open wider. "I'm supposed to go to Petland with Hillary to get some volunteer hours this afternoon."

Molly stopped listening after she heard the time. "Eleven thirty? You said it's eleven thirty?"

"I'm not even joking. I need to be at Petland at like noon." Flora came in and dropped onto Molly's bed. The cream-colored comforter was all twisted up, as if Molly had been doing yoga in her sleep. Flora was wearing her Saturday casual clothes, which still involved vintage black lace. Molly couldn't remember the last time she'd seen her daughter wear anything pink or yellow. She also wondered how a fifteen-year-old girl found so many syllables in the word "Mom."

"Um, okay. Just let me get up and dressed and…" Molly stopped struggling to sit up when she heard Flora gasp.

"Gross, Mom, you've totally got a hickey on your neck." Flora was nearly squealing by the end of the sentence.

"I do not." Molly put on her best mother's voice.

"Do too. Jamie, come see this. Mom's got a hickey."

"Flora, stop it. Jamie, I do not have a hickey." By now, Molly was standing up, more or less. She tried to push her bedroom door shut so that her son Jamie couldn't get in. He was three years older than Flora and at about six feet, two inches tall, he towered over his mother and sister. He pushed back against the door and slid his shoulders through.

"She's right, Ma, you do have a hickey." Jamie's voice was deep like his father's, and at times like this, she had trouble remembering which one she was talking to. Jamie and his father shared more than their voice. They had the same name: Wallingford Jameson Spencer.

Molly rounded the end of her bed and leaned against the polished maple bureau, staring into the mirror that hung on the wall behind it. "No no no no no," she whispered, fingertips touching the dark welt that was plainly visible right above the pulse point on the right side of her neck. Her shoulders were narrow and if her slim hips had started to widen recently, it was only to be expected when someone was forty-three years old.

"Um, I'd say it was yes yes yes, Mom." Flora flipped her long dyed-black hair and rolled her eyes.

Molly stared at her own reflection. Her cap of loose curls was going wild and yesterday's mascara was a shadow under her lower lashes. The light yellow nightgown she wore had only thin straps at the shoulders, so there was nothing to cover the mark on her neck. This was bad. Her cheeks bloomed bright at the thought of her kids seeing it, especially since she had no idea how it got there. She needed a shower and some time to think. She tried to say something, cleared her throat, and tried again.

"Okay, Jamie, you've got practice this afternoon, right? Can you go in a little early and take Flora to Petland?"

"Yeah, it's like in the totally opposite direction, but I guess I can drive her."

Molly made a face at him in the mirror. "If it's not too much trouble."

"Can I have some money for gas?" His wide brown eyes that were so much like his father's lit up when he found an angle he could use. She'd fallen for that look so many times.

"Take whatever cash is in my wallet." Molly sighed, and Jamie grinned at her. Fortunately his smile was his own, though she suspected he used it in much the same way his father did.

"If we're picking up The Princess I'm not going." Flora flounced off the bed and headed to the door. The Princess was her name for Jamie's girlfriend. Paige was tall, blond and athletic, the complete opposite of Flora and Molly, who were both petite and dark.

"Don't call her that," Jamie said.

"I can't believe you actually kiss her. I bet even her tongue's cold." Flora pushed past her brother and headed down the hall. He turned as if to follow her, then leaned back through the bedroom door.

"It's probably none of my business, Mom." That's as far as he got.

"You're right. It's none of your business. Thanks for driving your sister."

He gave her half a smile and closed the bedroom door.

Molly was glad when their bickering faded away. She sat back down on the edge of the bed and put her head in her hands, then groaned because she felt like such a cliché. She couldn't remember. She hadn't slept till eleven thirty in the morning since…well, college, maybe. And she had no idea why there was a hickey on her neck. Her stomach turned in on itself and she wondered if she was going to throw up.

The only noise she heard was the soft squish of feather pillows against sheets. She flipped the comforter around until it lay smooth and put both pillows behind her shoulders so that she was halfway sitting up. Her mouth tasted like she'd eaten a dead coyote and her stomach was still rumbling. When she shut her eyes, she saw a carved crystal shot glass filled with a golden liquid. Definitely tequila…maybe. That would explain her stomach.

Okay, this is bad. Forty-three-year-old mothers didn't go out and get sucked on. She raked her memories from the night before. There was the man. He was tall, handsome, definitely crushworthy. She couldn't remember his name. All she came up with was talking, even sparring. No kissing. No sucking.

Embarrassment over the fact her kids had seen the mark on her neck splashed over her like a bucket of hot water. She was supposed to be scolding them for getting hickeys, not the other way around.

Obviously, she could call Sam, who had been there for at least some of the shenanigans. That would mean confessing the big blank wall in her head, and it would give Sam the chance to crow over the fact that she'd finally gotten laid. *Oh God, had she?* Her stomach clenched as she rubbed her fingers between her legs. No. She didn't have the raw, morning-after feeling that only happened when it was really good or a long time. And it had been a very long time. She sniffed her fingertips and only smelled herself, then exhaled with relief.

Everything in her room was normal and tidy, the jewel-tone throw pillows from the bed stacked on the dresser and the nightstand clear except for the pair of gold hoop earrings she'd had on and a glass of water sitting in a circle of condensation. Yesterday's clothes made a puddle of green and black on the hardwood floor in front of the bathroom door. *Shit*. That outfit would have to go to the dry cleaner, unless she could press the wrinkles out of the suit. Worrying about her clothes kept her from worrying about bigger things, like whether the strange guy had slipped her some date rape drug and how close she'd really come to something horrible. Her breathing started getting shallow and her heart raced. Better call Sam.

Her purse was on the big antique buffet right by the front door, a piece of furniture that primarily worked as the family shit-catcher since she'd left the good china at Ford's. All of them dropped their keys and backpacks and bags either on or in front of it when they came through the door. Her wallet and phone were in the purse, right where they were supposed to be. The credit cards were still in her wallet. Okay, so Mr. No Name hadn't been a thief, at least.

"So tell your best friend all about it," Sam said as soon as she answered the phone.

"I was hoping you could tell me all about it. I seem to be missing some of the details."

"What are you talking about? Did you give him your phone number?"

Molly could hear Sam's youngest in the background asking her to cut the crusts off her peanut butter sandwich and had a moment of gratitude that Jamie and Flora could make their own lunch.

"I don't know. I was hoping you could remind me of a couple key things, like, maybe, his name, and whether you saw him slip me some kind of drug."

"What?"

Molly could hear Sam's mind switching gears.

"Um, yeah. I woke up this morning—well, actually, it was almost noon, and there's a huge hickey on my neck and I can't remember a thing. Oh my God." Molly bit her bottom lip to keep from crying. To distract herself, she glanced through the big front window. Her car was in the driveway, and while that was reassuring, it also meant she'd driven while, if not intoxicated, at least a little impaired. Damn again.

"Sweetie, I'm sorry. He seemed like a good guy. Are you, um, did you…"

"I'm pretty sure we didn't have sex. I mean, it doesn't feel like we did. I didn't even hang my clothes up, Sam." A weird little giggle punctuated Molly's comments, brought on by how unreal the situation was.

"It'll be okay. You should, like, call the cops or something. Go to the ER so they can test your, um…"

"Or take a hot shower and hope the blotch on my neck fades fast."

"Wait, no, you have to report this guy." The snap of the knife was audible through the phone. Sam must be cutting the bread right on the granite countertop.

"I don't know his name, I barely remember what he looked like, and I can't remember what happened. What am I going to report?" Molly perched on the edge of her old couch. If she tried to lean back, the fading springs would swallow her up, so she kept to the edge, knees together and elbows resting on her knees. One hand held the cell phone pressed to the ear, and the other cradled her chin.

"Well, he was…he said his name was…Fuck, I don't remember either." Dropping F-bombs in front of the children was a clear indication of how upset Sam was. They swapped details back and forth, but despite their efforts couldn't remember much about the man they'd met.

"It's useless." Molly didn't know whether to laugh or cry.

"I'm so sorry. It's all my fault." Sam sounded like she might start crying.

"Stop it. Stuff happens. I didn't get raped and the neck thing will fade. It'll probably teach my kids something about life to see me like this. Wait, I take that last bit back."

"Oh, your kids…"

"From now on, stick to lecturing me about my job, okay?"

"Sure," Sam said, her voice subdued.

Molly put her phone away and went to take a shower in the small master bathroom. First, though, she had to run down to the basement laundry room to find a clean towel since the linen closet was empty. Molly shook her head when she realized it was Jamie's turn to fold clothes. Just another opportunity to practice her mothering skills.

Half an hour later she was scrubbed and buffed and feeling marginally better. The fact that Sam couldn't remember much about the mysterious man was somehow reassuring, as if Molly wasn't his only target. While pulling on some clean jeans and a plum-colored turtleneck, she started packing away some of her embarrassment and dismay. Molly was very efficient at organizing her emotions and keeping them in neat little boxes.

She put on her favorite diamond earrings, and was scrunching some hair paste through her rowdy curls when she heard a sound, as if someone out in her bedroom had cleared his throat. She turned away from the bathroom mirror and leaned out the door, expecting to see a dark-haired stranger, her heart pounding so hard she could feel it in her ears.

Her bedroom was empty. Turning back, she grabbed hold of the vanity's edge. In the mirror, a man's face was next to hers.

"Aw shit." Molly shut her eyes, hoping that when she opened them things would be back to normal.

Praise for *Forever and Ever, Amen*:
"A twist on angels and demons, with a little vampire. It was quite fascinating and not what I expected. If you are looking for a heartfelt contemporary romance with a touch of the supernatural, *Forever and Ever, Amen* is just for you."—Satin Sheet Romance

In the mood for more Crimson Romance?
Check out *Drive Me Sane* by Dena Rogers
at *CrimsonRomance.com*.